FATMA
A LOVE STORY

JOEL RANDY BLAKE

My name is Randy Blake and most of what I am about to tell you is true. Some of the names have been changed because I couldn't remember the correct ones and some of the dates are wrong. But the facts included are true, some of the other stuff might be questionable. Confused? Welcome to my world as Jim Reeves might croon.

CHAPTER 1

"JESUS CALLS"

"I don't want to, mama," I pleaded, trying to hold back tears.

"You gone do what I told you," she spat the words at me, and I knew what would likely follow. Not a rational discussion of my seven-year-old wants and needs, but a swift slap to the side of my head.

"Please don't make me, mama," I begged, tears while I stuttered over the words that gushed out of me.

"You goin' back in that bedroom with Uncle John. You gone close that bedroom door, and you better not come out till I tell you to."

I moved toward the front door, but the old fat woman was quicker than she looked. I could feel her nails digging into my skinny bare arm, the hate blazing in her black eyes. I was squalling hard now. Squalling was what always evoked the same response. "You better stop that squalling right now or I'm gonna give you something to squall about." She was a firm believer in the fact that you couldn't hurt a child by beating him too much. I could never understand years later how a guy as smart as Dr. Spock could leave this important doctrine out of his book on child-rearing.

"Never mind, mister. I'm gonna drag you back there myself and make sure you touch him in that bed," she said more like a promise than any kind of hollow threat. I think that was when I first realized I hated her.

Uncle John never moved when she forced me to touch him. The stench was stifling and putrid, and it hung over the hot bedroom like the permanent smell of grease you find in a Georgia diner. I don't know why I was surprised. He'd been dead for almost two days before anybody checked on him. He was wearing a stained wife-beater shirt, dingy grey boxers that had once been white, and black socks almost to his knees, no cover on him.

He didn't get much attention except around the first of the month when his check came and my aunt Dessa or Uncle Tobe needed him to sign it. I don't think Uncle John was related to them. They just took him in one day out of the goodness of their hearts, so everybody said.

"If you don't touch the dead, then you'll have bad dreams. This is for your own good," she explained as she forced my hand against his unshaven jowl that was cold and fatty. The feeling of that cold leathery sandpaper flesh evoked memories of hog-killing days. And also, memories of pork rinds with hairs still on them, but we ate them anyway. I hated killing hogs. And now fifty years later I still wake up in the middle of the night, in a sweat, remembering touching a smelly old pig of a dead man.

There was lots of squalling that day from aunt Dessa,

Uncle Tobe, Charlie (who was a year older than I was), Sarah who was about fourteen, Doyal who was two years older then Sarah, Benny who was about twenty ("and not right," as my mama always said) and D.C., who was twenty-four and fortunately was home during this time of sorrow. I always thought D.C. worked out of town, but later I realized he was in and out of jail. He always smelled of homebrew and to his credit, he always tried his best to keep Benny away from Sarah whenever he came home. But, sadly, D.C. was often away. Food was plentiful whenever someone died, and the two-bedroom blockhouse was loaded with good smells and well-wishers who really didn't know much about Uncle John, just that his passing was a great loss. And he would not be forgotten soon. Mann and Walden Funeral Home had finally taken the body away in a large black Cadillac hearse, so I was happy about that. Probably the only time Uncle John had ever ridden in a Cadillac.

I usually liked these gatherings because of the fried chicken. There always seemed to be fried chicken served at these special events but for us kids, the fried chicken is what made these events special; most nights we just ate corned bread and buttermilk. Sometimes I would put some chopped onions in my corned bread just for a little change. My mama wasn't much of a cook even if we had food to cook. Sometimes she'd fry potatoes and we'd eat those with pork and beans. We didn't mind the bad food too much because we didn't have much else to compare it to aside from the funeral fried chicken. Being poor wasn't something that we fretted over because for the most part we just didn't know. We were not the kind of family you would find fighting over assets in a probate court. We had nothing and nobody we were related to had anything nice enough to want.

Later both of my sisters ran off and got married. Donna was fifteen and my aunt Alice forged my mama's signature to make everything legal. Sandra was sixteen when she left to get married. Once again Aunt Alice did her duty. I was never sure why they left home so young. I sometimes wondered if maybe they finally figured out we were poor. There wasn't much money to go around in our house but at least we always had enough for three packs of cigarettes a day for my mama. My daddy (deddy as it was more commonly pronounced by poor people) did the best he could, working six twelve-hour shifts every week at the Bibb Manufacturing Company in Porterdale. There was never enough money to support a family even though my mama worked for the Bibb too. Nobody ever got rich working in a cotton mill except the person who owned it. Pop supplemented our income with a small family business- the manufacturing and distribution of corn liquor. Every now and then I remember seeing Sheriff J.T. Walls come to the house, handcuff my father, and guide him into the back seat of the cruiser. My mama always explained that he had some friends who worked at the Sheriff's office and he was just going to visit them. It was mighty nice of Sherriff Walls to give deddy a ride. My pop always slipped him a quart of his best chartered whiskey after he made bail and the Sheriff would bring him right back home.

My family made the best chartered whiskey in the state, aged for years in barrels to give it that golden reddish tint and a taste that would "bite your tongue, warm your belly and make your dick get hard," a sales pitch I had heard many times (and the Madison Avenue folks would have been hard-pressed to top that slogan). People paid more for the chartered whiskey, even though we didn't even own any barrels to age it in. The family secret was to cut off some small limbs of a fruit tree, trim the bark and drop a few small sticks into a half-gallon Ball mason jar filled with the white liquor and bury it in a hole for a few days.

When you pulled it out of the hole and shook it a little, the golden-reddish bead sparkled and increased the value of the whiskey by fifty percent. Our stuff would hold its bead for a long time too. That's when you truly knew you were holding a quality product. I often wondered if burying my mother in a hole for a few days would improve her quality.

Charlie and I were best friends, some days. Other days we hated each other. My first memory of visiting him was when I was around five years old. I had to go to the outside bathroom and he was ordered to show me where it was. If you've never experienced the shock and trauma of chickens pecking you on the asshole when you were doing number two, then there is no way I can adequately describe the horror. I often wondered if Charlie experienced a similar level of shock when I kicked him solidly in the balls to curtail his laughter.

Sarah was the family flower, the most beautiful girl I ever met. I can see why they always joke about cousins marrying cousins in Georgia. She was tall and thin with long dirty blonde hair. She had blue eyes and had a quick smile that could warm your heart more than that charted whiskey ever could. I never liked to see her cry, especially when I heard her tell her mother "Benny won't leave me alone." Aunt Dessa always had the same response, "be quiet or your deddy will kill him. Do you want to see that?" Sarah always said "no, mam" but I knew she was wishing Uncle Tobe would kill him as much as I did.

Doyal was a couple of years older than Sarah. He had acquired a taste for homebrew at an early age, so he dropped out of school when he was sixteen to help on the farm and concentrate on perfecting his distilling talents. The family grew or killed most of what they ate. My aunt and uncle both worked at a box manufacturing company, but like us, they never had much money. Aunt Dessa, short for Odessa, was just a plain woman, not too fat, sandy thin hair graying earlier than it should have; she had a big mole on the left side of her mouth and she always had a large dip of chewing tobacco below her front bottom lip that would bulge out. She wore large glasses, so her eyes were hidden most of the time. She might have been pretty as a young girl, but that train had left the station quite a while ago. Uncle Tobe was a large man, six three and two eighty, hardened by the depression years, still bitter, and only allowed things to be done in a certain way: his way. Everything about him was big. His teeth, nose, lips, ears, head, and most of all his temper. He was crazy from religion, embracing it to cover a dark youth that nobody wanted to talk about. He did not drink anymore, proving sometimes lack of alcohol makes some people mean.

Doyal was a typical sixteen-year-old, awkward, and preferring to stay to himself. He had some friends, the Minor brothers who hung around him a lot. They were bad news, especially when they were drinking. They were always smiling. I never understood why people with such bad dental problems insisted on smiling all the time. They had such a reputation for trouble that most stores posted signs that said, "No Beer Sold to Minors." Doyal and the Minors died one Friday night on our road, Irwin Iridge Road, near the Yellow River bridge. I always thought it was Irvin Bridge Road until I was seventeen and they put up a few road signs. My mother, the dumbest woman in the world, had always called it Irvin Bridge Road.

Nobody said so, but I am sure there was alcohol involved in the wreck that took Doyal and the Minor boys, Dwayne and Wayne. There was fried chicken but not as much grief as when Uncle John died.

Benny Banks was the worst limb in the Banks family tree. We will discuss him more later. D.C. was tall and handsome and reminded me a lot of Sarah. Later the word I would use to describe him was charming. His muscles were well developed from years of being dragged through many fields by stubborn mules who could never seem to understand which way to go when you said gee or haw. I still don't know which word meant right or left. I do know that D.C. never understood which way was right himself. I was a little older when I finally understood why D.C. was away so often. He was kind, but that didn't matter too much to anyone outside our house. To the rest of the world, he was just bad. Uncle Tobe took Charlie and me along to visit D.C. in the Fulton County jail once. Through the bar's Uncle Tobe asked, "D.C. what have you done?" Uncle Tobe's words sounded tear-stained, reminding me of D.C.'s constant alcohol-stained breath, whenever he was home.

D.C. slightly shook his head from side to side and said "deddy I was just getting a little bit and the next thing I knowed, she hollered rape. Everybody said she could be frigid like that." I later understood that some women could be frigid and never warm up to a couple of men like D.C. and another friend from one of his many alma maters, stopping to offer to change a flat tire for her on her way home from work at 11 pm, then tying her up and gagging her and raping and sodomizing her for two days in a homemade fish tent on the Yellow River. Frigid. I had spent many wonderful days and nights on that Yellow River with Charlie, just fishing and talking about how our lives would change as soon as we were old enough to drive and get a car. After I heard D.C.'s story, the river itself seemed frigid to me, no matter what time of year it was.

The jury ignored the fact that this twenty-year-old girl, who was working the night shift at Dairy Queen to help support her husband and eleven-month-old baby girl, had been asking for it when she got that flat tire on that dirt road, just a mile from her trailer. Some juries are unfortunately funny like that. I never saw D.C. again.

Aunt Dessa and Uncle Tobe did the best they could, I suppose. He was the stern disciplinarian and she was just the mother who loved her children no matter what their shortcomings were. That was the kind way to see it, but in all honesty, I lied when I called him a disciplinarian. He was a mean bastard who beat his wife and children with a vengeance for any minor infraction. He was also a man of God. All my life I have discovered that some of the meanest people alive were people of faith. I am convinced they never felt as bad about Doyal's passing as much as they did Uncle John's, who was not even related to them. I guess the grief was less for Uncle John and more for the loss of the fifty-one dollars a month he received from the Social Security Administration.

My granny lived on ten acres in a two-bedroom house with a large porch where she liked to quilt. When she was not working in the garden or around the barn, you could usually find her on the porch with the large frame lowered almost to lap level so she could create patchwork wonders. We lived next door in a Jim Walter home "finished to whatever stage of completion you desire" as the ad said. This meant a handy person could save a lot of money by doing some of the work himself. My father was not handy. We lived in this modern shell of a home for seven years with no sheetrock in the interior and no indoor plumbing.

Granny knocked on the door lightly and yelled for me and my brother Earl who was sixteen months younger than I was. He looked just like my mama. Black hair, black eyes, and an expression that screamed "I am the second stupidest person in the world, next to my mama." My hair was so blond it was nearly white and his was black. I was a foot taller, but people constantly asked if we were twins, because this idiot woman always dressed us alike. I'm pretty sure she did this until I was in the Navy and finally the government stepped in and made her stop.

Speaking of military service…I am always reminded of my cousin Junior who lived just a couple of miles up Irvin (Irwin) Bridge Road. His mother Mary Lou was my father's sister, who had married a man named Willis

Wilson. As long as I knew Uncle Willis, he had never worked. They farmed like everybody else in the area and somehow that seemed to get them by. Junior was their pride and joy. He was called Junior not because he was named after Uncle Willis, but because that was the name on his birth certificate…Junior Lamar Wilson. Junior was not a junior, but his parents had always liked that name. I'm not sure if he joined the army when he turned eighteen or was drafted. Toward the end of his two-year stint, he was stationed in Germany for six months. When he returned home, he talked with a German accent for years. Later, I would feel sorry for the Viet Nam veterans who came back, suffering from PTSD and other problems. But at least I was glad they never were burdened with speaking with a Vietnamese accent for years.

Conyers was the county seat (like a small capitol of a county) of Rockdale County, appropriately named because about half the land around us was flat rocks. It was a flat plain building surrounded by a sorry excuse for a fence. The building seemed like the centerpiece in a graveyard of fence posts, each propped up with rocks around their bases to hold them upright. The posts were barely able to support the few strands of rusted barbed wire to contain the pathetic few cows, a mule, and a goat or two. Why fence in the flat rocks when there was nothing there the animals wanted or needed? Why not just fence in the area with dirt, trees, and grass? Once while in grade school one of my teachers mentioned to the class that on a drive over the weekend, he saw fence posts propped up with rocks. Everyone in the class laughed except me. The heat rose from deep inside me and I turned red, all the while trying to become invisible like that guy on TV.

It was about a two-mile walk. Granny never owned a car or even knew how to drive one. As we walked, she sang a couple of hymns I recognized. She was a big woman, part Cherokee Indian with long black hair that never turned grey up until the day she died. I was older when she passed, so I didn't have to touch her. I could always tell if it was a special occasion when we walked to town. I guessed we must be going to church, or going to a funeral. These were the only times she dabbed on a little Avon Crème Sachet. It gave her a kind and gentle smell. My mother used that too, but when you mixed it with the strong smell of unfiltered cigarettes, the effect was totally different. I am sure that even now as my mother sits in one of the seats closest to the fire, the devil is screaming constantly "what is that God Awful smell?!"

The preacher who did the graveside service for Uncle John was what we called a hard-shell Baptist preacher. Rumour had it that shithouse rats used to talk about how crazy he was. He was at his finest during the foot washing services when he explained in a kinder and a gentler voice about Jesus' belief in serving others. These were good services because I could understand what he was saying, and there would often be a fried chicken church dinner afterward. The dusty graveside ceremony took place outside the peeling white, one-room Mt. Zion Baptist Church. Pastor Prentiss cried a lot when he was really feeling the presence of the Holy Spirit and on this day the Spirit's presence must have been powerful. He had to dry the tears from his eyes and the spittle from his mouth several times before he could continue. I heard him say later that he loved funerals because people always listened better at a funeral. About once a month Preacher Prentiss would hold prayer services in my Granny's house. Charlie and I always liked to watch through the window of Granny's bedroom/den because people would speak in tongues and some would even pass out. Religion was a serious thing back then, maybe not so much because people like us were all that worried about the afterlife, but because it was something to do that was free.

It was a hot afternoon for a funeral and all the old people were working the wooden handled fans supplied by Mann and Walden Funeral Home pretty hard. It was much later that I realized why Mann and Walden supplied these fans to almost every church in the county. It was a good place to find old people that make new customers. Prentiss was sweaty and his suit and shirt were almost soaked from the afternoon July sun. His suit was big but his body made it very tight (probably from the fried chicken) and straining from his exaggerated movements and gestures toward Heaven. His gray hair was thinning and combed straight back and held in place by a generous application of Brylcreem hair cream. Sometimes through the years, he would lean down to talk to me quietly and I'd be able to smell something besides the hair cream. His breath had a presence that couldn't be ignored. It reminded a lot of Doyal's breath after he'd come back from making trouble with the Minor brothers. There were definitely traces of alcohol in his breath but I couldn't tell if it had a chartered tint to it or not. Please don't think that everybody in Rockdale County was a drunk; It only seemed to be the ones I knew or was related to. Prentiss would frequently say "fighting off the devil is terrible work" and I believed that as much as he did, so I didn't begrudge him those minor transgressions. He was always available to visit the sick and infirmed, especially if he thought the customary dollar bill might be exchanged.

My mother always did her part to instill religion in my brother Earl and me. She would take us to Sunday school every week to emphasize the importance of religion in our lives. She never went in, just sat in the car and smoked. She always dropped her short cigarette butts in a small pile outside her car in the church parking lot. I guess you could say she was devout.

Prentiss forgot the ashes part of the ceremony, so he leaned a little too heavily on the dust art to make up for it. Looking through that cloud as it finally cleared, I got my first glimpse at mortality, the meaning of life, and what was lying ahead. Standing near the grave was a spray of flowers with a sky-blue plastic toy princess phone attached to the styrofoam that supported the flowers. A shiny white banner was attached to the top bearing the phrase "Jesus Calls."

CHAPTER 2

WPLO

"From fifty-nine on the dial, this is WPLO, a broadcast service of Plough, Incorporated...."

Some debates will rage forever. There's Darwin's theory about how life began and evolved. He thought a couple of slimy things crawled out of the brine, shook the water off, then one mounted the other and they started making other slimy things. Some people think God reached down and picked up a handful of dust and created man; Although more than likely he was either digging at his ass or picking his nose and rolled something around until it looked like man). And some scientists think before man started drawing in caves, different animals mated until they got it right (or wrong). There will never be a debate about when my life started.

My life began at the WPLO AM radio station in the 805 Building on Peachtree Street in downtown Atlanta. My life before that day was nothing but shame and excuses, and suspicious looks from mothers who didn't want their daughters to spend time with me. They could see that I came from nothing and would always be nothing. But now I was the youngest disc jockey on the number one country music radio station in the world. I was twenty-two years old and exactly where I wanted to be. There were a couple of exotic stops in my timeline before I arrived at WPLO, but this is where my life left the starting gate.

When I was fourteen Santa Claus brought me a portable radio for Christmas. It could be powered through a wall plug or batteries that I could rarely afford to replace. I would sit and listen at night to John "records is my middle name" Landecker on WLS in Chicago. Sometimes when the weather conditions were just right, I could hear George Michaels on WABC in New York. I sounded like a black southern kid with a twang when I would sit for hours and imitate them for my own amusement. In the fantasy of radio every DJ was rich, handsome, and irresistible to beautiful women.

My life was a country song.

> **PRODUCTION NOTE:** *It is imperative, if you have never heard it or even cared about country music, that you find a copy of "He Stopped Loving Her Today," by George Jones and listen to it carefully. It is the quintessential country song.*

Every year WPLO delivered "The Shower of Stars," at various shopping centers around Atlanta. The biggest stars from Nashville happily appeared to sing all the hits from a stage on a flatbed truck set up in the parking lots. The crowds were mammoth. It was all free, so the neighbors could be a little scary at times. These were my people!

At my first appearance at one of these shows, I think it

was at South Dekalb Mall in Decatur, I met Loretta Lynn, the reigning queen of country music. She brought her little sister along, Crystal Gayle. Crystal and I were about the same age so she and I gravitated toward each other and had some time to talk backstage (or backtruck I should say). She wasn't a star yet, but she killed them later on. I am not an adequate enough writer to describe her beauty, so just look at some old pictures for a real treat. After each show ended, we all headed to one of the ballrooms of the Biltmore Hotel to party with the stars the rest of the night. Country stars were appreciative and accessible.

About the third night of my first year at "The Shower of Stars," A major country star was one of the artists appearing. He's dead now, so I won't defame him. Besides being an incredible performer, he was a lady killer and a party animal. We were all standing around, or maybe staggering was a better word to describe the circumstances. He was feeling no pain (high as a Georgia pine as my deddy used to say).

"I would drop down on my knees and suck Porter's dick just to see what Dolly's pussy tastes like," he declared loudly and sincerely. I often wondered later what went through his mind immediately after that remark when he turned and faced a twelve-year old girl. (As a side note, Dolly swore she and Porter never did it. Porter often swore they did it all the time.) It was an eventful week. My first marriage ended on the fourth night when I threw my wedding band out of the car window on the way home. I had married my high school bitchheart because that's what you did back then when the girl was in the family way.

Seems like her name was Beelzebub or something like

that. This night she was at her finest. She hated radio, she hated me and she hated Jeanne Pruitt. Jeannie took a strong liking to me because I told the greatest jokes all night long. She was at the top of the charts and the top of the world at the time with a little song called "Satin Sheets." She offered to take me on tour as an opening act to warm up her crowds. My dear wife was convinced she wanted me to warm up something else, and I gladly would have. All this from the beautiful creature who wouldn't give me any on our wedding night (a trip to the local justice of the peace is still a wedding). She was already giving it to some other guy; So why did she care? She did give me a wonderful son, Jason. I will always be grateful to her for that.

I soon met Ronna Jones who was five years older than I was. Ronna stole my heart as only a beautiful blonde, brunette or redhead could (or even one of those cancer women wearing a scarf on her hairless head). We met at a charity auction I was asked to MC at Lake Lanier Islands. Skip Carey, the Braves announcer, was also invited. Ronna was best friends with a girl named Robin who was Skip's girlfriend. I don't think his wife knew about Robin. She was striking and kind and he was the biggest asshole I had ever met. He kept Robin in tears most of the weekend, just because he could, I guess. Ronna was the loving mother I never had. Whatever I wanted; she was agreeable. She was a cutie and usually followed my lead. We were inseparable and I proposed several times. She never agreed to marry me, even though she might have wanted to. I still had a wife hanging around. Gomorra was her name I think. I always knew this beautiful blonde would eventually be my wife. And then I met Elain.

"What? I'm busy." I answered the phone in the production room. It was the receptionist named Jean Raven, a dark-haired Jewish girl with full lips and a body that dreams were made of. She wouldn't give me any either.

"You have visitors, sweetie."

"How could I have visitors? I'm not even supposed to be here." I worked 7 pm to midnight on the air, but Bob Byrd, the production director (the guy who made commercials during the day) left early because he wasn't feeling well, so I was filling in. Marty, the copywriter, had also left early because she wasn't feeling well. I suspected they were both feeling much better now. They were in love. Bob used to take me for beers at the Prince George Inn on a side street a few hundred feet from the station. He took me after he got off at five and before I went on at seven. Many times, I would stop by the Varsity (a world-famous Georgia burger chain), pick up two chili dogs and two tall cans of Schlitz beer and consume all that the first hour I was on the air. Remember, I was young, but I was already a pro in many categories. Back to Bob. A different time, at a homo bar one day Bob asked me if I'd ever thought about having sex with a man. I said no and the subject never came up again. We still drank there often. They were some of the nicest homos I had ever met.

"She seems to know who you are and what you're doing with the talent show. You really need to see her. She's almost as pretty as me." Being the youngest guy on the staff, I usually got stuck with all the unpaying gigs, like the WPLO talent show for future stars.

As pretty as Jean Raven? "In that case, I would be happy to speak with her. Bring her back to the FM studio."

WPLO FM was progressive Rock and the studios looked like the bridge of the USS Enterprise. Space age and exciting. My second choice to being on the radio was to captain the Enterprise. Besides my duties on the country station, I was one of the voices on the FM side. It was totally automated (except one of the times I was fired and had to work 8 pm to midnight live a few months on the FM side. Just a misunderstanding. Then they hired me back on the AM side when things cooled down).

With all due respect to Patsy Cline…I fell to pieces when the door opened and Elain Lively, her husband Ronnie, and their daughter Lori Lynn walked in. I once interviewed Barbi Benton when she had recorded a country song that Hugh Hefner, her boyfriend, was promoting. She didn't look human in person because she was so perfectly beautiful. But Elain made me forget all about Barbi. She was a model, five ten, of course blonde hair, green eyes, and displayed a wicked smile because she knew exactly what she was doing to me. She was wearing a dark green jump suit with a matching wide headband. She reminded me of a fashion magazine cover. I don't remember what he looked like or the daughter.

After introductions, she said, "We're here so you can make our daughter a star." Lori Lynn was a beautiful child and had inherited the same confidence her mother wore like a cape. "Lori Lynn, sing something for him." She broke into song and for a ten-year-old, she sounded like she'd already been a star for most of her life.

"She is really good," the response of an idiot who couldn't take his eyes off her mother. "But I don't know what I can do. I'm just one of the judges of the contest."

"You don't have to do anything," Elain assured me. "We just wanted you to meet her."

"I am truly impressed," I said. A man who makes his living talking could think of nothing witty or smart to say. "Keep in touch. And if there's ever anything I can do, please call me." Ironically, Lori Lynn never made it (although she did win the talent contest). But Elain had three other children who did ok. Jason Lively was in a movie with Chevy Chase called "European Vacation." Robin Lively had a solid movie and TV career. And as of the writing of this book, Blake Lively is doing pretty well, too. Elain always loved my last name and said if she ever had another daughter, she was going to name her Blake.

The next day when I came in and checked my mailbox, it was mostly the same thing…see me, jc, another see me, jc, and another see me, jc. I wasn't in too much trouble because when I was, my boss Jim Clemmons always left a note that said see me immediately, jc. There was a strange phone message with no name or number that said simply "will meet you out front at midnight. We need to talk." Great. Probably the husband of some lonely woman I had played a song for and used her name on the radio. I had no intention of getting ambushed by some snuff queen's husband. I was a little rattled all night, but like you always do when you have a blister in your mouth, you have to stick your tongue on it repeatedly to make sure it still hurts. I had to know. I walked out into the parking garage under the building, walked to the corner of Fifth Street and Peachtree Street and peered around the corner. There was a white Ford Fairlane parked on the curb in front of the building. I waited and watched. It looked like whoever was in the car was constantly adjusting the rear-view mirror, probably to see if someone was coming up behind the car. I later realized she was touching up her makeup.

I rapped on her window and she jumped. She rolled it down and said, "my God, you scared me."

"You know this is not the nicest neighborhood in town," I cautioned. I wasn't kidding. During my exile to the live show at night on WPLO FM, I used to watch sting operations out the window overlooking Fifth Street. A good-looking female cop would stand on the street and guys would pull up and try to pick her up, then after a secret signal from her, all you heard was woop woop. Blue lights and a trip to the jail at the taxpayers' expense. Once I overheard Uncle John and Benny discussing a trip downtown and how they had picked up a lady of the evening, morning, and afternoon. They still laughed about what a good job she did on both of them for three dollars. And they were perplexed why both of them had a sore throat for a few days. There's a visual for you. But, back to something beautiful, a love story.

"I'm not complaining, but why are you here double parked on Peachtree Street at midnight," I really wanted to know. Also, does your husband own a gun?

"I came to see you."

"Is this business or pleasure," I really wanted to know that. Is little Lori Lynn in the back-seat ready to sing another song?

"I'll let you decide that." She laughed like she was genuinely glad to see me. "Nothing complicated. You just seemed genuinely nice the other day and I just wanted to talk to you again."

"Tell you what. I know a great restaurant over on Piedmont that's open late. I usually go there after work (liar, liar pants really were on fire. I usually went to a honky tonk bar). Let me get my car and you can follow me."

"Can I park and ride with you?" I got in her car and gave directions to the parking garage. I was so glad I was driving a new Firebird. She was impressed.

We spent several hours at a Waffle House just talking and laughing. Elain told me her marriage was over because Ronnie had cheated. She was devastated and had prayed and prayed for God to help her make the right decision about her marriage. And then, he sent me. I told her about my wife Sodom and her indiscretions. I admitted to being as much at fault as her, but my mistress was radio while her paramour was flesh and bone. Well, okay, there was Ronna, but my wife had opened Pandora's box first. I forgot to tell Elain about Ronna. Who's Ronna?

We shook hands at the end of the night and gave each other a friendly hug. For the next five years I would often ponder pouring gasoline over Elain and me, then setting fire to it just to cool us down a bit. I'm lying again. It was much more than five years.

Production note to whoever is writing the movie script for this book: Insert Olivia Newton John's song "I Honestly Love You" here.

It was late as we were leaving the Waffle House at three in the morning, our regular hangout a few nights a week. She ate all that greasy stuff like a horse and still stayed thin. Nothing tastes better than soft lips marinated with hash browns, onions, and chili. There was a lovers' rain falling, soft, slow, and steady, and cold enough to need someone to help keep you warm.

"Y'all married," the wrinkled old night clerk at the Mimosa Motel on Highway 41 (Cobb Parkway) asked, and then took a long draw off her Pall Mall and blew a cloud toward us, causing Elain to back away fanning the air.

"She is." I smiled.

"That'll be sixteen dollars cash," she frowned, never once weighing the moral implications of accepting the cash from two people who were about to sin their brains out.

After weeks of kissing and slapping my hands away from her breasts, Elain agreed we should get a room just to nap. She had to drive all the way back to Powder Springs and I had to drive all the way to Conyers. So, it just made sense that we take a nap…for safety's sake. The Mimosa was a one-story motor court, frequented by truckers and married people who were married to someone else. It was winter and just as cold on the inside as the outside when we entered the room. I turned on the AC/heat unit sticking out under the window and it started rattling warmth. We never turned the lights on. If we had, we would have seen maple furniture, scarred by cigarette burns on every flat surface.

"No, the clothes stay on." And it sounded like she meant it.

"Let's just get comfortable so we can fall asleep," I reasoned. We took our clothes off but she left her bra and panties on. I kept my underwear on. She finally let me take her bra off and we laid there cuddling and touching. When I couldn't stand it any longer, I reached down and tore her panties off. When I entered her, all I heard was "my God, my God. Thy will be done, thy will be done!"

There were two rough white towels, never touched by fabric softener, and she used them both after she showered, complaining about the roughness, and smiling at me the whole time. I never complained about using a towel that had already caressed her.

"Why are you smiling?" I asked. She couldn't stop.

"Same reason you are, baby. I am in love. I never knew what being in love was really like until I met you." She was looking directly at me with those soft blue eyes.

"Anything you'd like to tell me?"

I walked to her, removed the towels, and lowered her back on the bed. "You already knew I was in love with you from the first day, didn't you?"

"Yes." She admitted and smiled again.

"Please don't ever leave me," I said.

"I will never leave you," she promised. "This will never end."

If God had had the foresight to introduce Adam to Eve at the Mimosa Motel instead of in that garden, things might have worked out better. There are times even now I pass by the Mimosa on Highway 41. It has a new name now, fresh paint, a newly paved parking lot, and a new roof. I always slow down, not knowing whether to smile or cry, but then I usually cry.

Country Charlie Pride had agreed to be on my show that night. His promoters dubbed him Country Charlie Pride and didn't put his picture on his first album. Nobody knew how the neighbors were going to react to a Negro singing country music. Charlie was one of the nicest people I ever met and his music bridged that gap with country fans everywhere in no time It was my mother's birthday that night. I don't remember which one, but she was a huge Charlie Pride fan. I always called her Gladys since I was a small child and realized I hated her. If I were an abused wife, I'd have two black eyes every day. I just kept going back for more punishment. Charlie readily agreed to call her and sing happy birthday to Gladys. As the shock wore off and she told him how much she appreciated it, he told her she was welcome and mentioned what a proud mama she must be.

"Charlie," she said almost tearfully, "I am. When Earl called me last week and said he had passed his GED on the second try, I just had to call and tell everybody I know."

PRODUCTION NOTE: *Please insert "Just Between You and Me" by Charlie Pride here. It fits my mood at this time.*

"Why didn't you tell me you had Donna Fargo in the studio today? I would have come by," Big Jim Morgan, the overnight guy and my best friend complained. We had already had a couple or three, and some beer.

"She's a little bitty thing," I explained, "so there wasn't enough for both of us to look at. And besides, I couldn't take a chance on having you there. Just suppose she was mad at her husband and wanted to get even. If you had been there, she might have chosen you instead of me."

"Good point," he conceded. "I would have screwed you over too, given the same circumstances."

Donna Fargo had the number one song on the charts at that time, *"Happiest Girl In the Whole USA."* She was a baby doll and America's sweetheart, and a former teacher.

Big Jim Morgan was six two, two hundred pounds, black curly hair, dark eyes, and was always happy. We looked like Mutt and Jeff. I was five eleven, thin, with brown curly hair trying to go blonde again, blue eyes, and I rarely smiled due to my happy childhood. He and I shared a love for beer and hard fiddles in country music. He had confided in me once that his wife had this nasty habit of banging every guy she ever worked for, no exceptions.

> **PRODUCTION NOTE:** *Please play "It Was Always So Easy to Find an Unhappy Woman 'Til I Started Looking for Mine" by Moe Bandy.*

We would later commit a felony together. But let's not dwell on that now. In my mind this is a love story.

Elain and I were headed to Panama City for Memorial Day Weekend. I will admit, for a married woman, she had no trouble getting away to spend time with me. Still, she was married. If you've ever been in a relationship like that, it can destroy you to watch the one you love to get up and go home to someone else. I was the other man. We fought almost all the way to the beach, then finally pulled over behind a fruit stand in some little town in south Alabama and made love in the car.

"Sometimes I hate you," she confessed. "But I always love you." And that, friends and neighbors was the story of our lives.

> **PRODUCTION NOTE:** *You can always find a country song to mirror your life. Johnny Rodriquez's "Just Get Up and Close the Door" seemed to say it all during this relationship.*

And why is it when you are feeling miserable and low, sad songs seem to help?

If you've ever seen the movie Urban Cowboy, then you will understand when I tell you Gordon Dee's Place on Moreland Avenue was nothing like Gilley's Place. Gordon had bounced around with his band all over the southeast and finally got his own place, a converted semi hub. Jim, Ronna, a date Ronna found for Morgan and I used to go there as often as we could (and whenever I felt Elain wasn't going to track me down). I spent lots of time hiding from the love of my life.

The first time we walked in, we sat on an elevated area with a few tables that had a good view of the stage. And a good view of the men's room. The door was a plain piece of plywood with a spring like you'd find on an old screen door that closes it automatically. The thing about the plywood was it didn't fit too well, so when the door opened, it left a wide crack on the right side right in front of the commode. All night long we could see bare-assed guys taking a crap through that crack. You couldn't see that at Gilley's place.

On this night, the Paul Peek Band was appearing before Gordon Dee. Paul only had one eye and wore a black patch where his other eye should be. His rendition of Willie Nelson's song "Blue Eye Crying in The Rain" usually brought the house down. To quote an old newspaper writer from the Rockdale Citizen, "a good time was had by all." And then Elain walked in.

"You followed me?" Why I sounded guilty, I don't know. She was the one who was married. She looked really good, all dressed up.

"I didn't come by to make a scene. I just came by to tell you that it's over. This is what you've chosen, so I want you to be happy," she said calmly and quietly then turned and headed toward the door.

I told the group I'd be right back. I followed her out to give her a piece of my mind, all the time feeling like the entire place was watching me through a crack in a plywood door.

She rolled the window down and said, "it's over, baby." She started the car. I felt like a surgeon had removed my heart before they were sure the donor's heart had arrived and might not.

"Don't leave," I said.

Her eyes were hard when she turned to face me. "Get in."

I knew I was surrendering my soul and I was happy to do it. Who needs a soul, or sanity for that matter, when you are hopelessly in love? I knew my days were numbered at WPLO. I was a wreck and just didn't care anymore. I will put it in perspective for you movie lovers. When Glen Close boiled the rabbit to get even with Michael Douglas, I didn't relate to him. I was the rabbit. I was relieved when Clemmons said he had to let me go. The damned radio show was taking up a lot of time I could have been using to finish destroying my life.

Someone once told me all the nutcases and losers eventually wind up in Florida. They are so mentally lost that they think the warm weather and the water will actually solve their problems. So, I headed to Florida. I had called Ben Hill, a guy I used to work with back in Monroe, Georgia when we were both getting started. He was program director at a Rock station called CK101 in Orlando. The studios were in Cocoa Beach. He said come on down and we'll make a spot for you. I cried all the way there. I didn't even tell Elain I was leaving. If I had called her, I would have never left. I had to get away from a woman I could not leave.

PRODUCTION NOTE: *"If You Leave Me Now" by Chicago would fit nicely here.*

Three months of women in bikini's, crystal clear blue water, white sand and Thursday nights at George's Galaxy Lounge for the "sensuous banana eating contest" (always won by the gay guys), station trade tabs to drink for free and lots of seafood did absolutely nothing to change my mood. I was unhappy. I called Ronna and she was there the next day. We spent a beautiful weekend together and I asked her to marry me. She said yes. She left Sunday night and I turned in a notice, packed my car two weeks later, and headed north toward Atlanta.

It was raining hard the night I got to Atlanta, but I stood at the payphone anyway and called Elain. She met me at the Mimosa Motel.

CHAPTER 3
FATMA

FATMA ALWAYS SMELLED like Tube Rose or Bruton snuff, depending on what the peddler had on his old Easter egg green pickup truck when he came around on the third of the month. You could hear the old Chevrolet Apache rattling the minute it turned down the dirt driveway that was shared by four different houses. I could never comprehend his monthly punctuality until someone told me later that the welfare checks were received on the first of the month, cashed by the second and people still had a little money to spend on the third. Fatma was a widow and had four children, five if you count me, and she received seventeen dollars a month from the county. She and her children worked on Jones Hortman's farm for basically nothing just to keep food on the table and a leaky often patched tin roof over their heads.

I am sure that God created niggers so white trash like Jones Hortman would have someone to look down on. "Couple y'all niggers get up on that roof and get them shingles nailed down before this rain messes up all that hay," Jones ordered Harry, Fatma's husband, and a slim boy everybody called Slim to head up the ladder.

"Mr. Jones. It's awfully wet up there and slick," Harry protested mildly. The roof was twenty-five feet high with a steep pitch.

"You get your sorry asses up there or hit the road." Harry knew he couldn't afford to lose what little money he made, so he started up the ladder.

Nobody saw Harry start to fall it was raining so hard, but those who saw him hit the ground headfirst said he didn't have time to suffer. This was how Fatma became a widow.

The next day Jones stopped by her house and told her how sorry he was and couldn't understand why Harry just didn't wait for the rain to stop before he started up that ladder. He pressed a roll of bills in her hand as he was leaving, totaling thirty-two dollars, and told her she didn't have to make any more payments on the house. She and her young'uns could stay there if they liked. She almost pointed out to him that they had been making payments of fifty dollars a month, three years past the agreed upon terms when they would own the house. But Jones kept collecting and Harry kept paying in spite of her protests.

In 1917 in Portugal the Virgin Mary appeared to three children and predicted miracles. The locals used the name Fatima for the Virgin Mary. This was a favorite story of Fatma's mother, so when she was born, she was named Fatima. When her mother went to register the new birth at the courthouse, they spelled it Fatma and when the child first started school her teacher called her "Fatmaw," disregarding the child's attempted explanation of the error. The other children all laughed and the name Fatma (pronounced "Fatmaw") stuck.

Most rural people I knew lived by the good book, The Farmer's Almanac, and planted by the moon phases. First crops were always planted on Good Friday, even when it came a couple of weeks early, running the risk of losing seeds, fertilizer, and abundance when the crops came in. Losing labor was not much of an issue; it was one of the few things most people could afford to lose and replenish. The Almanac was a guide for living and I learned early that the other Good Book was more of a guide for dying, a road map to where you were headed at the end of it all. A road map without all the difficulty of refolding. You lived, then you died, rarely leaving any marks behind in the Georgia red clay to declare you ever existed. If you were lucky, there was enough to buy a piece of granite with your name and dates chiseled on it that proved your existence.

"You goose lickin' it, Randy," she explained to me patiently, her front left cheek bulging slightly with a dip. If you gone pick cotton for Mr. Jones, you got to clean it all out of the boll. You don't, Mr. Jones won't pay you."

I liked working beside Fatma and her children. I made hardly any money, but I enjoyed the family atmosphere. They smiled a lot and obviously loved and protected each other. Something I had never experienced as a child. My mother was cold and mean. I never had a single memory of sitting on her lap or getting a hug. Fatma hugged me often. I always gave her what little money I made, and she protested every time. She cried and hugged me every time I put three or four dollars and change on her kitchen table. It was well spent. Then every month on the third when she bought Sugar Daddy's for her four children in addition to her snuff, she always bought one for me. My fingers would hurt and bleed from the hardened cotton bolls, but I didn't mind. I was happy being around her family. Little Harry was seventeen and couldn't wait to leave home, so he complained a lot. The twins Samuel and Jeffrey were fifteen and Jasmine was twelve, a year or so older than me. I would discover at an early age that I had a thing for older women, especially one as pretty as Jasmine. She had caramel skin, dark eyes, and pearly white teeth. She smiled at me a lot.

"You ain't never had possum?" Jasmine asked, incredulously. Little Harry had caught one in the garden where Fatma grew vegetables all summer and greens all winter. It did smell good.

"Looks greasy," I said uncertainly.

"Every animal you eat is greasy," she smiled. "Have you ever seen a pig that wasn't greasy? Every part of it is greasy, except maybe the oink," she laughed. "Randy, it's your turn to ask the blessing," Fatma reminded me.

We all bowed our heads and I said, "dear Lord, thank you for all the blessings you bestow on us every day and thank you especially for this greasy possum we are about to receive."

Everybody laughed and Jasmine kicked me under the table. It felt good. The possum was greasy, but hot and tasty, and the laughter and conversation filled me with happiness. Comfort food? Maybe not, but the warmth of this family was comforting. After dinner Fatma made everybody start homework, including me. We attended different schools because blacks and whites were not allowed to mix in the early sixties. Fatma was a smart woman, self-educated, and wanted a better life for her children than what she had. After an hour or so of homework, she read from the Bible for a few minutes. She considered this an important part of education. Usually, it was dark when I started home, thinking about Jasmine more than conjugating sentences and multiplication. Fatma was probably sitting by the wood stove having a pinch of snuff and humming songs like *"What A Friend We Have in Jesus,"* rocking a little and praying to God to get her through one more day.

"Where you been, Mr. Encyclopedia, up there with them niggers again?" My loving mother demanded. Once again, God made niggers so white trash would have somebody to look down on. She called me Mr. Encyclopedia because pop had bought a set of World Book Encyclopedias and a set of Science Encyclopedias from a traveling salesman and insisted I read from them both on a regular basis. I started to like it, and once attempted to share what I had read with Gladys, but she had no interest. I hadn't gotten to the L's yet and Lucky Strike cigarettes were the only subject that interested her. Pop often reminded me he was still making payments on the books, so I felt some obligation to read them.

"Why do you call them that? They're nice people." She just shook her head hopelessly, lit another Lucky with a wooden kitchen match, blew out the thick blue smoke in my direction and left the room, even though I could still see her through the sheetrockless studs, sitting by the kitchen stove, enjoying her cigarette. Pop was convinced the Russians were really coming and spent his off time when he had some down time in the family business, planning and building bomb shelters. He would come up with a new idea to protect us from the nuclear bombs the Russkies would be dropping any minute. We had dug a hole for a septic tank, but he never got around to buying what was needed to finish it, so we still had a two-holer outhouse.

He had covered the septic tank hole with plywood that had since rotted through and on this day was explaining his latest idea to me. "I got some plastic and we're going to put that up all down the hallway and in one of the bedrooms and the bathroom, which I'm gonna finish because we'll need that since we won't be able to go outside until the radiation has all died down. It's not the explosion that gets you, it's the radiation," he reminded me once again. We had had this conversation a few times, usually after he finished watching the evening news on TV. "I've already started stocking up on pork and beans (the family favorite) and bottles of Pepsi. If we have enough time, we'll fill up some water jugs. We can make it on that, but we'll have to be careful with the supplies."

"Ok," I said, knowing it was fruitless to point out his former projects that had not worked out. I wondered if he had considered whether or not the plastic would stand up to the thousands of degrees of heat generated by a nuclear bomb. We started nailing up plastic. We were gonna show that Krewsheff fella a thing or two. Later when inspecting our supplies, I noticed four half gallon jars of corn liquor in a corner, probably to be used for celebration once we brought the Russians to their knees. His Browning "Sweet

Sixteen" automatic shotgun and three boxes of shells were also stored near the door for quick access. How are you gonna kill any Russians with that little 25 caliber automatic, Mr. James Bond?

Pop was self-educated for the most part, but he was still just a dumb country boy who did the best he could. He was a handsome man even though his hair was thinning a bit. I could tell by the way other women looked at him that he was handsome. I could never understand why he didn't pursue some new opportunities, knowing what he had at home. One of the saddest moments of my life was when he was describing Bing Crosby in the movie White Christmas. "Bing was singing the song *'White Christmas'* and then took his pipe and tapped the tune out on Christmas ornaments on the tree. It was perfect," he smiled, impressed by Bing's musical talents. Despair and shame were my constant companions as a child. I still loved him. He only beat me when he had to, not because he liked it, like Gladys. I think it was the only way she could express her own unhappiness.

Jones Hortman was married twice. He was a hard man, a hard drinker, and a heavy smoker who had to have everything his way. He was short and stout, maybe five five, with a full head of hair, dyed bottle black except for the quarter inch at the bottom of the hair. That part was white every time I saw him. Lifeless eyes, milky blue like an unpolished gemstone, and no lips at all. He owned over two hundred acres of good farmland his folks had left him, but even that was never enough to keep his first wife happy. She left one day after seventeen years of marriage. She either walked away or someone picked her up. She was never allowed to drive and even if she could, she never had access to a vehicle. Nobody was sure, but it was obvious she was so ready to leave her husband that she left all her clothes and family pictures behind. Maybe she didn't want to be reminded of her former life. There were no children involved, so it must have been easy just to leave an unhappy situation. She was never heard from again.

Jones was quite sure she would never come back. Six months later he married a girl whose father worked for him. She was eighteen and he was forty-one. No one questioned the validity of a new marriage even though a divorce was never sought.

Things were less complicated then for better or worse. His new wife was named Carmen, and she was not only young, but she was pretty. People speculated her father and Jones had reached some kind of deal to pressure the girl into marriage with a much older man. The father was seen loosely spending money for a few months after the happy occasion, a luxury he could never afford before. She always looked ashamed and haggard whenever her family and friends were allowed to visit. Her long dark hair often tangled and she seldom smiled as she did before. One cousin said Jones forced her to do things that were unpleasant and often painful. This was not part of her wifely duties as she understood them. But she was young and inexperienced in the ways of the world. And she knew better than to complain. Jones was known to take the strap to his young wife when she did things to displease him, or if he were drunk and just felt like it.

The marriage didn't last long, probably a couple of years, and the ending was less vague than that of his first marriage. Jones came home early one afternoon and found Carmen naked in bed with a twenty-two-year-old who worked on the farm for Jones. He shot the boy six times with a Smith and Wesson .38 revolver in front of Carmen. He slowly reloaded and she knew she was next. But just for good measure, he put five more shots into the boy and saved one in case things got out of hand.

The casket was closed for the funeral because she had been beaten so badly with the pistol that Mann and Walden couldn't restore her face enough so that the mourners would even slightly recognize her. In our parts, she was his property and he had every right to kill her. He was never charged with a crime because it was not a crime to protect your property or to kill a cheating spouse in the state of Georgia.

Jones spent eleven dollars on a custom frame and mounted the bloody pistol in it without even wiping it off. It's probably still hanging over his mantle if he's still alive. Mean people usually live long lives. The ones who deserve it never seem to get what's coming to them.

We were picking cotton when he walked up, just having a good time. It got quiet when everyone realized he was in the field. "Jasmine, you are filling out in all the right places," Jones said and I was sure he was mentally licking his lips. "I might have to find some things for you to do up at the house," he smiled knowingly.

"You'd better not touch her, you son of a bitch," I threatened. I never saw it coming. He hit me so hard between the eyes with his balled fist that all I remembered was pain and blackness. My nose still has a hump where the break was never properly treated.

"You get your little nigger lovin' ass off my property. And if you ever come back, I'll blow your brains out," he promised.

I pointed at him as I staggered away and said "you better not touch her. I'm warning you. And I'll be watching. And a little more advice for you, too, don't ever mess with somebody who's crazier than you." He just shook his head slowly.

It was the first time I was ever fired. Lost my first love and my first job on the same day. I never saw Jasmine or Fatma again. Someone told me a few years later Jasmine had a baby when she was fifteen. She never said who the father was, but the baby was real light-skinned.

Sometime later, because time didn't mean much at my young age, little Harry walked into our yard. He told me his mother had died suddenly of a heart attack. "Too much heat," he speculated. "You know how hard she worked in the garden. Didn't matter what time of year it was. I just wanted you to know. She always thought highly of you." I nodded and wondered if she'd be able to get her snuff in Heaven, where she was surely bound.

"Thank you for telling me, Harry. I always thought a lot of her too." I turned and walked into the house without even asking about Jasmine. I spent the rest of the day lying on my bed, crying.

I was the only white person at her funeral, sitting under the green awning that said "Lackey Funeral Home" with her children. The old preacher who did the graveside ceremony had thin white hair, maybe looking like one of the bolls I had goose licked. His upper teeth were all gone and his bottom teeth jutted out, but he seemed sincere and smiled a lot and talked about what a better place sister Fatma was in. Everybody said amen to that, so I hoped there was something to it. It seemed to always be hot when I was young, with summers would last most of the year and the winters always seemed harsh but brief. I was happy for this sweltering day, hoping it looked like I was sweating instead of fighting unstoppable tears. There was fried chicken and lots of other good food after the service, but I had no appetite. I started walking home, wondering, "Who's gonna love me now?"

PRODUCTION NOTE: *"Mansion on The Hill" by Hank Williams.*

CHAPTER 4

WQXI, QUIXIE IN DIXIE

Gary Corey was program director of WQXI, one of the hottest Rock stations in America. He looked a lot like Hal Holbrook, square chinned with a thick mop of hair, no lips, and a sincere stare that said you can believe anything I say. He was around forty years old, but like Hal, he had that 'I am much wiser than my age' look. Like me, he didn't smile often, and infatuated by his on-air characters like Willis the Guard, I was in awe. This giant, this legend had taken the time to call me, after I dropped off a tape, to discuss the possibility of working for him.

The station was state of the art, just like its on-air persona, with complete walls bearing Warhol-type modern art with the likenesses of people like Elton John, Jim Morrison, Jimi Hendrix, and no cans of soup. No expenses had been spared in these posh digs on the second floor of the Tower Place Building in Buckhead, the real money area of Atlanta. In radio, this was the top of the heap, the pinnacle for all wannabes like me.

"Here's what I need, someone to do my swing shift. That means you can work any shift I throw at you whenever I need you. Your content is good, so you have the talent to work any shift here."

"More, more, tell me more about how good I am." I thought to myself as I couldn't help but smile. "Finally, somebody who loves me!"

"Your stuff is funny, timely, and relatable. But I need a little more pep from you. I don't care if you have to take a hit of speed before you go on the air, I just need more energy from you. Do you think you can do that?" Corey asked almost blandly.

"I can do it," I assured him. "In fact, I'll take some speed right now just to prove it, or heroine, no maybe not that. I don't like needles."

He chuckled slightly. "Do you know Coyote?"

"Not personally, but certainly I listen to him all the time." Coyote McCloud worked 6 pm to 10 pm and owned the night ratings.

"Yeah, you and every other thirteen-year-old girl in Atlanta," again a slight chuckle. "See Joanie. She's the one with the big tits right outside my office, and don't tell her I said that. She'll get you an entrance card, employee forms, parking information, a secret handshake, and whatever else she thinks you need. It's Monday. I'm putting you on the air on the simulcast show, both AM and FM starting Saturday morning, so learn everything between now and then. Joanie will call you with your weekly schedule every Friday morning. I'll be listening Saturday morning, so make me proud." He shook my hand and turned away. Over his shoulder he said "don't plan anything on a personal basis. You'll be working six days a week. You belong to me now." Just like that the meeting was over.

"I heard what he said about my tits," Joanie said, almost complaining. "Dirty old man."

"Maybe he just appreciates real beauty," I tried to cover for him.

"You are so sweet. Too bad you're so young." Joanie was maybe thirty-five, five-seven, thin, large (you already know), professionally dressed, makeup perfect, a real looker. I later discovered she was a stoner, but just a sweetheart. Always ready with a sincere smile. She actually ran everything in the programming department; she was really smart. "Call me first if you need anything. If I can't handle it, we're in trouble." She handed me a card and wrote her home number on the back. "Anytime, day or night. Don't call when you're drunk and just want to talk about my...." She smiled and gave me a welcome hug. In all the time I knew her, I could never say anything negative about her.

And that was the beginning of the next best five years of my life. I couldn't wait to call Elain, then I remembered we were taking some time off. My suspicions were she was trying to put her marriage back together since she suggested it. Anytime a woman suggests "time off" or something about "needing space," rest assured, she's banging someone else. I always felt sorry when a guy said something like we're taking a break. Yeah, I thought, she's taking a break alright: trying to break some guy's thingy with her vagina. Admittedly these types of thoughts did not support my own mental stability. Didn't matter. The lid had been torn off my mind and I was on my way. I needed to concentrate on my career anyway, so even though I missed her, I was determined to dig in and set the world on fire. I was young and on 790, WQXI, Quixie in Dixie. I could almost see it, John "Records" Landecker and George Michaels frantically trying to tune the station in on their little transistor radios just to hear me, their panties wet with anticipation back at my old station.

I put on one of the station shirts in the car that Joanie gave me and then called big Jim. "What's up, stranger?" I hadn't seen him or talked to him in a while. "What are you doing after ten o'clock tonight? We have some celebrating to do."

"What are we celebrating?"

"My newest job on Quixie."

"No shit!" He was impressed. "I'll be at the Casa Blanca just after ten. I'll be the handsome guy with his hands on Karen's ass." Karen White was the bartender there. She was a babe and she knew it, but she was smart enough to not give too much attention to guys like me. The Casa Blanca lounge was located on the bottom floor of the downtown Hilton, facing Courtland Street. Chairs and booths were dark red leather, the bar was mahogany and there was no piano with a black man named Sam playing sad love songs. I couldn't believe that detail in the decorations had been overlooked. Who wants to look at an old black guy when Karen's around anyway? Funny. I always worked my drinking schedule around her work schedule as often as possible.

Rod Stewart's *"Tonight's the Night"* started automatically. "QXI and 94Q. This is Randy Blake…" I can't remember what else I said, but I hit the post perfectly. That's when the DJ talks at the beginning of the song and finishes just before the singing starts. It takes some work to do that, but once you've been on the air for a while, you know exactly how long it takes to say a thought. I was recording (scoping) the show. The microphone automatically starts the cassette recording when it's turned on and stops the cassette when the mike is turned off. So, you can listen to all your live breaks and not have to listen to more than a few seconds of music. I listened to the first show on the way to the Casa Blanca Saturday night. I was ready. Unfortunately, again, Karen was not.

"Why is it when I'm juggling two women, I get all kinds of offers, and the minute I hit a dry spell, women won't give me the time of day," I lamented after a few at the Casa Blanca.

"They can smell it on you," Morgan said dryly.

"What?"

"Yeah, they can smell it on you, and then they know you'd be a good mate. I think I read that in some medical journal. It's true."

"I've missed you, Morgan. Nobody is as full of shit as you." We laughed our asses off. "When have you ever read a medical journal unless it was one featuring an article on how to get rid of the clap?"

"So, where's the tall blonde? I figured she'd be here tonight." Morgan probed.

"We're taking a break. And she doesn't drink, remember."

"Yeah, that's right. I forgot. She still crazy?"

"Yep, no improvement there." We both laughed again. "Hey! you're talking about the love of my life, pal." We laughed more. "Yeah, she's still crazy," I admitted. We laughed harder.

"They all are." He leaned over and clinked my glass with his.

"You've got to see the station. Give me a few days and I'll give you a tour. It's unbelievable. Not like all the stuff at PLO that looks like Marconi's garage sale. Jean Raven still there? Tell her to call me at 790, WQXI.," I said in my deepest voice and we laughed again. I had missed laughing for a while. I never seemed to realize how much I needed a friend like him until we laughed together.

"You guys want another round? Last call," Karen informed us politely. I usually don't like dark haired women, but she was elegant, with a hint of Asia in her dark eyes. She was tall, thin, and always smelled good. She wore exceptionally long skirts almost split up to the ass as per company uniform. 'Sultry' and 'intercourse' are the words that she brings to mind, in that order.

"Of course, we want another round." I pointed to the logo on my shirt and asked "Did I mention where I'm working now?

"About twelve times," she smiled. "I am happy for you. I was worried about you for a while. I could tell you were unhappy. You seem much better now."

"I'm going for broke, so just be honest with me, Karen. I won't remember anything bad you said to me tomorrow anyway. It's obvious I'm in love with you, but the harder I try, the less you want to give me the time of day. What am I doing wrong?"

"You really don't know?" She whispered. I shook my head slightly. "A woman can tell when a man is in love with someone else. Call me when you get over her."

I dropped money on the table and left. What a buzz kill. I guess they can smell a broken heart on you too.

Production note: *Play that Ten CC song "I'm Not in Love." And bring me another glass of hemlock.*

Coyote McCloud was about thirty-five years old, shoulder length ratty blonde hair, friendly, open smile, a perpetual three-day stubble, almost emaciated. As far as I could determine, his only sustenance was unfiltered Camel cigarettes. If you never saw him pause to light another, you'd probably assume he found the cigarette that burns forever. Mrs. Coyote had proudly delivered him six children and Mr. Coyote had about a million teenage girls willing to bear his next child. I envied him. I had heard him talk sweetly and patiently about family things to his wife when she called on the hotline. He loved his wife and family.

Corey had me doing 10 pm to 2 am after Coyote every night because the spring ratings were starting soon and everything had to be stabilized to maximize those. Quixie always participated in the Ramblin' Raft Race in the spring, a drunken trip down the Chattahoochee River on homemade rafts with about five hundred thousand of your closest friends. The race got lots of publicity and always delivered a strong spring book, which translated into big money. It eventually got so big, it had to be canceled. The city and county didn't have enough manpower or resources to adequately maintain control. If you ever attended one, you will readily attest to the fact that it was out of hand.

When I was in high school, we built a raft and entered

the race. It was the thing to do back then for kids my age. About halfway down the race, a drunken girl in a bikini fell off a neighboring raft and went under. They finally got her back on the raft but she was not moving. One of the idiots on our raft shouted, "float her over here and we'll all fuck her before she gets cold!" Thankfully, she finally sat up and asked for another beer. The older men on the raft were not amused. Our raft is probably still at the bottom of the river and we had to walk to get to the end of the race where we caught a shuttle back to our cars.

"Quixie," I answered the request line.

"Hey, baby." I recognized the voice immediately.

"Well, well, haven't heard from you in a while. How's your husband?" I tried to sound cold and aloof. She hung up. I was surprised at how I was holding it together. It reminded me of chopping cotton. The blisters were painful but once they healed a couple of times they became hard and it didn't hurt anymore. Maybe the heart is like that; but then again, cotton doesn't have nice breasts or really long legs. Just a thought.

"Why do you always hurt me?" She called back five minutes later.

"I can't talk now. I'm really busy. And it's finally over. Don't call me again." I felt Stronger after saying that.

"It will never be over," she said calmly and hung up. Dammit. She beat me to the hang up. That was one of our most popular forms of foreplay.

When I got to the parking deck, she was leaning against my car. I unlocked it and told her to "get in." She never said a word until we were inside the room at the Mimosa Motel. The rooms were old and smelled like cigarette smoke and broken vows, but the sheets were clean. One side of the bed was propped up on a stack of red bricks. I'm sure whoever left the bed in that condition has one hell of a story to tell.

"I've missed you, baby." And then she started to weep openly. So, did I.

In Vegas they have a saying, "the next best thing to winning is losing." The premise is you're still in the game. I was the other man, but I was still in the game. I also knew that one day we would be together forever. There was no doubt in my mind that this woman loved me as much as I loved her. We were just in all the wrong places at all the wrong times. There was no doubt in her mind that I would die for her if asked; she would die for me under the same circumstances. A love like that begs the question of why we still aren't together. To be entirely honest, that's a question I don't have an answer for. Have you ever seen buzzards working over roadkill, pulling stubborn pieces from the carcass? They're scared away by a car, then return to the dangerous area to rip away more pieces until it's picked clean. That was the kind of love we had. Even now I would lie down on that road and enjoy every piece she ripped from my heart, all the while just enjoying the undivided attention she was giving me while she did it.

PRODUCTION NOTE: *Good place here for "Love Hurts" by Nazareth.*

I remember reading the encyclopedia back when I was younger and being hung up on the clinical example of insanity. It wasn't running around doing crazy things to get attention or acting like you're trying to expel demons from your body. The encyclopedia described it in terms of legal strategy. Colloquially, insanity was explained as doing the same thing over and over again expecting different results every time. Being with Elain reminded me of that definition, although it was a bit different for me. The kind of crazy she had me sick with was doing the same thing over and over again and loving the results every time.

We were in bed at my place in the Riverbend Apartment Complex, the place to live for young professionals in Atlanta. It was also the finish point for the Ramblin' Raft Race. I always loved Sundays there. There was beer by the pool, greasy stuff smoldering on the grill, and women looking for mates, not husbands. Elain was always in church on Sunday. I would stare at all the other scantily clad women and think about Elain.

My apartment was her creation. She did all the decorating and bought all new furniture to her taste. After all, it was her home away from home. She also picked out most of my clothes, including designer suits. We were an impressive pair by any standards. "We have to talk," she whispered.

"What now. We need another break. You need some space?" I was getting angry.

"I'm pregnant. And before you ask, it is yours. I have not been with another man since that first time with you. I know you think Ronnie and I are still a couple, but it's just not true. The kids love him. They need him."

I didn't feel trapped; I felt locked out. "Elain, what do you want to do? I would marry you tonight, but you're still married. What do you think he's going to say? Are you two going to raise my child?"

"I don't know what to do. I need for you to decide." She sounded helpless.

"We have two options. You can divorce him immediately and I will marry you, or you can get an abortion. Those are the only two options right now."

"I can't do that to my kids right now. As much as I love you, they are my life."

"Enough said. I'll find a place," I said stoically.

The procedure only took a couple of hours from start to finish. We got a room so she could rest and I spent the day with her, holding her and comforting her. She cried most of the day. When I dropped her off at her car, she got in, and before she closed the door, she said "you killed our baby."

I rarely answered the request line or the hotline after that when I was on the air. The hotline was a direct line that ignited a red light instead of ringing. It was strictly for management and significant others to use. I didn't want to talk to either. She left messages at my apartment but I never returned her calls. She came by a few times but I never opened the door. She kicked in the glass sliding door once out of frustration, or just to show she still loved me. Morgan and I were both working mostly days at that time,

so we spent most evenings at the Casa Blanca Lounge. I can honestly say we were not drinking any more heavily because of these recent events. Heavily was where we started a long time ago.

"I think you and I need to talk. I brought you two a beer on me. We won't be long, Jim," Karen said. We were the only two people in the bar at the time; most people are not getting sauced at two thirty in the afternoon. She led me to an empty booth in the backroom behind the bar. I figured she was about to try to sell me some Amway products. And I would have bought them readily. "Look, it's obvious I made you mad when I said something about your being in love with another woman. You're cold toward me and I hate that. I thought we were friends. Honestly, I thought someday you and I might even end up together." I could tell this was hard for her.

"You were right. I was in love with someone else. I guess it threw me for a loop because it was that noticeable," I admitted. "I am finally over her," I lied. "I'd like to be friends with you, but I will never fall in love again. I'm just being honest." Why did I want to cause pain to someone who cared about me? Because I could, I guess. Maybe I felt like it was my turn.

"What was that all about," Jim asked. "She looks upset." I sat down with a cold straight face.

"She's upset about all the demeaning remarks she's heard you make about women. She's finally had enough. I'm welcome here, but she doesn't want to wait on you anymore." I was half joking and half lying and he seemed upset by it. "Ok, I'm lying. But I am offended by those remarks."

He recovered and said "good one. Brace yourself. I owe you."

"Wouldn't have it any other way."

A few minutes passed. Finally, I said, "Look, I know I joke about stuff at the wrong time and sometimes about stuff I shouldn't be joking about anyway. This just caught me off guard. Karen is two months late and she's upset." I lied again but this time for some space instead of his reaction. Morgan got quiet and when he broke the silence, it was like he was walking on a thinly frozen pond. "What are you gonna do?"

"Find somebody else to fuck. You know I don't like fat women." He shook his head. I felt bad and told him I needed another minute with her.

I pulled her back to the booth we were in before and told her how intimidated I was by how beautiful she is. That line never failed. "I would like to take you to a nice dinner soon, and we can just talk. I'll tell you all the mistakes I've made in my life up until this minute, and you can just hold me and let me cry on your shoulder."

"I'd like that," she smiled.

PRODUCTION NOTE: *Disco was hot, so please insert Thelma Houston's "Don't Leave Me This Way."*

Nuances. They're what make life so complicated. Nuances define the difference between love and hate, the difference between sadness and happiness, and the difference between fiddles and violins. There are no nuances when it comes to a broken heart; it's all or nothing.

Ronna Jones forgave me again. Maybe she was the one for me, but I intended to take it slowly. Life was fun again, hitting the clubs, dancing to the Bee Gees, drinking and loving. Everybody dressed up and showed their best stuff. Laugh about disco if you want to, but what a great period. People were dancing on a big scale again. Women love to dance. Enough said.

PRODUCTION NOTE: *Alicia Bridges' "I Love the Night Life."*

Elain sent letters to the radio station constantly. Every time I found one in my mailbox, I tore it to pieces and never read it. I started parking down the street at Lenox Square, so if she ever showed up, she couldn't get to me. I left by secure entrances whenever I got off the air. It was a massive complex, so it was easy to avoid her.

"Why don't you two just get married?" Joanie asked. "You at least need to talk to her. She leaves a message with me every day. She's really upset." I was in the jock lounge, doing some show prep and nursing a hangover.

"She's crazy. And so am I. Do you really see that going anywhere positive?"

"No, but I feel sorry for her."

"Feel sorry for me," I pleaded. "Have you ever heard of a mercy…?"

She turned and started walking away, but I heard her say "I see who the real asshole is here." I knew she still loved me though.

I started answering the phones again and she called and said, "please don't hang up." I had not spoken to her in six months. "My divorce is final in two days. We can get married the day after it's final." For over five years this had been all I wanted. Now some of the open wounds had finally healed. "We can move to L.A. like we always talked about."

"Good luck, Elain." I hung up. There was a giant scab over my heart and I had no intention of picking at it. I was in love with a bartender whose only complaint was I worked too much and needed to spend more time with her. Life was getting sweet again. (Note to all bar managers and owners. Guys hate male bartenders. When I'm pouring my heart out, I want somebody soft to listen, not some guy busy scratching his nuts.)

Ronna left me after I admitted I was in love with a dark-haired girl. She found someone else who was happy with just one woman. I did not wish her well. Had I taken her for granted? Yes. Had I treated her badly? Yes. But I still needed her to catch me when I fell.

Morgan and I started drinking about 2 pm at the Casa Blanca. I don't remember what day it was. I wasn't much for remembering special dates like birthdays, anniversaries, or the day; life as you know it ceased to exist. When the bar closed at 2 am we walked down the street toward our cars. We stopped to take a leak on the MARTA bus lot. The bus doors were all open so we stepped inside one and realized you didn't need a key to start some of them. The worst thing about being in radio is you start to think the life you're living is real. It is far, far from reality. We were about to get a good dose of reality. We managed to get the bus through downtown Atlanta. We stopped once at a bus stop because there was an old black man standing there. We opened the door, and when he saw us grinning, he just turned and walked away. For some reason, we got on I-20 East heading toward Conyers. Who says you can't go home again? We took turns driving, but either way, apparently our driving might have been somewhat erratic. Some meddlesome person had made a call to complain about a weaving bus.

I was driving when we got off at West Avenue. We decided to ditch the bus on the access road at the Holiday Inn. As I looked left, I saw a sea of blue lights coming down the hill. "Must be a helluva wreck," Morgan noted. We had no clue they were after us. I made a left turn on the access road and stopped near the Holiday Inn. All we could see were blue lights behind us.

The Rockdale County Sheriff's deputy motioned for me to open the door, which I did. "You a little lost, ain't you?"

"No," I said innocently.

"Well, first of all, MARTA don't run out here."

"I know. We're just dropping the bus off at the Holiday Inn as a favor. The guy who was supposed to drive it out here got drunk while we were playing pool, so we're just helping him out." I have no idea where that story came from. I had an uncanny ability to tell a deep straight-faced lie without a moment's notice.

"Let me see your license," he said politely. We're going to take you and your buddy there to the jail and straighten all this out."

"Is it ok if I run into the Holiday Inn to take a quick leak? You can hold my buddy hostage."

"Yeah, go ahead, but hurry up."

I called Karen from a payphone and got her machine. I told her where we were and where we were likely headed. I needed her help even though I had no idea what that help might look like. Everybody at the jail was really nice, except for the female hog impersonator in the deputy uniform. They of course couldn't reach anybody at MARTA at this hour to confirm or discredit our story. They never even asked us if we'd been drinking. Hog woman was not buying our story for a minute, but the decision was made to let us go and get in touch with MARTA later in the morning. As we were leaving, hog woman looked at us and said, "don't worry, I'll be seeing you two real soon." Sometimes it's better to just keep your mouth shut and keep moving, but remember, those of us who make our living talking never know when to quit.

"Obviously, you don't know who we are," Big Jim said as we left. Unfortunately, she made it her business the next day to find out exactly who we were, and then things took a turn for the worse.

Karen was waiting, thank goodness. "Got an interesting call from the Rockdale Sheriff's Department a little while ago. Did you steal a MARTA bus last night?" Corey asked. I had been dreading this call.

"Technically, yes. But I can explain."

"Don't bother, Blum wants to fire you immediately." Gerald Blum was the General Manager. "I talked him out of it for right now. Don't talk to anybody, especially anybody in the press. You'll be getting a call from an attorney shortly. Do whatever he says." He hung up. If you've ever seen the TV show "WKRP in Cincinnati," Blum looks just like the general manager on that show. (The TV show was based on Quixie.)

"Everybody's laughing." I just wanted you to know." Joanie called to check on me. "Just do what they say and everything will be just fine." God Bless this angel. "Corey has scheduled you for some extra shifts. He said we might as well make some lemonade out of this turd. If you need anything, I'll be around. Just call. If you want, you can come by tonight and we'll smoke a joint or something." Why do chicks love outlaws? I promised myself I'd start smoking dope just so I could visit Joanie. Only kidding. I was getting all the comfort I needed from Karen.

And the media went crazy. TV, newspapers, and other radio stations, except WPLO, who refused to run the story. Morgan still worked there and they felt it was better to keep quiet and hope for the best. We found out on the six o'clock news we'd been indicted for stealing a MARTA bus. I called the attorneys immediately. There were three of them now. He said bail had already been arranged for Jim and me. "We'll meet you in the morning outside the Fulton County Jail, they'll book you and you shouldn't be in there too long. We are also representing Jim. Don't talk to anybody." I suspect the attorneys notified the press about what time we'd be turning ourselves in. Hey, they have to make a living too. It was standing room only outside the jail and we two dumbasses were the stars.

I must say the Rockdale Sheriff's Department was a much better experience than the Fulton County jail, even with the hog woman's lack of a sense of humor. They printed us, took our pictures, and put us in a holding cell with nineteen black guys. We were there until early evening. While swapping stories with the other hard-timers, it was obvious our story was the most popular, even though we heard some horrible stories about why many of them were in the same cell with us. And by some astounding coincidence, they were all innocent just like Jim and me.

Our attorneys picked us up and took us to a nearby restaurant to go over what would happen next. Their plan was to go before the court and ask the charges to be dropped because no one could verify that we stole the bus. A week later that's exactly what happened. The judge agreed and dropped the charges. The attorneys explained that within six months or so, the prosecutors could possibly ask for a grand jury to be convened. Then the prosecution might try to go after us on other charges, but we would cross that bridge when we got there. For the moment we were just grateful to be able to take a sigh of relief.

That night on the evening news we discovered that a special grand jury had indeed been convened right after our court appearance. Exactly what we were afraid might happen happened and we had been indicted for receiving stolen property. We breathed that breath of fear and anticipation right back in and headed back to visit our friends at the Fulton County Jail once again. Maybe they'll serve fried chicken for our homecoming celebration.

The media would not let the story die. Every night on every TV station we were the big story and the newspapers just couldn't get enough. Corey was delighted. The station's call letters had never been on the front page of the newspaper or on the lead story of the evening news. Blum didn't fire me, but he did give me some nasty looks on occasion. WPLO didn't fire Morgan. Why would they? They knew nothing about a bus story. Jean Raven never called to console me either.

The phone rang at home. "Are you okay, baby?" I hung up immediately. Even now many years later I still think about her. Thank goodness we never got married. You cannot maintain any sanity when the passion level is that high.

Just before the trial, round two of the media frenzy exploded again. We had to re-live the nightmare over and over. Our judge looked like Woody Allen without the humor. Small man with thick black glasses and a heavy gavel. He threw the book at every person he sentenced before us. I was convinced if the worst happened, I would try to run out of the courthouse and escape into nothingness. He smiled when our case was called, which was the worst thing he could have done. All I heard was "I sentence you to one year." He hit the gavel and mumbled something about probation. I was shaking when the attorneys took us into the hall and explained we would serve a year on probation and not have to go to jail. We would not even have to report monthly to a probation officer. And since the judge had allowed us to use our first offender rights, the conviction wouldn't show up on our records if we stayed out of trouble while on probation.

I was happy and almost called Elain. But we decided to celebrate instead with Karen at the Casa Blanca Lounge. She wasn't working, but I needed a drink. And with a little persuasion, Morgan agreed to come and celebrate. Karen didn't drink much so she took Morgan to his house and me to her apartment. I'm pretty sure I proposed to her. I usually do that when a woman is nice to me or gives me good service at a restaurant.

By the end of 1978 I had a hard time working at Quixie. I was after all on probation and had to stay out of trouble for a year. Drug use was openly accepted at the giant rock station and I was scared. Early in 1979, I resigned. I had no regrets. It was an incredible ride and I was lucky to know when to get off.

> **PRODUCTION NOTE:** *Please insert Eric Clapton's "Cocaine" here.*

Just after the new year, Morgan and I were both asked to MC the A.S.S.I.E. awards. Gordon Dee said the awards ceremony would be held at the Silver Saddle. We never turned down an opportunity to drink and chase women. The initials stand for Atlanta Society of Sick and Incompetent Entertainers. They recognized the accomplishments of local artists and entertainers for the previous year. Morgan and I were totally surprised to also be among the honorees: Dumbasses of the Year. I gave my trophy to Karen as a token of my undying love. If she hadn't over served us, this achievement might not have been possible.

Karen left me shortly after that. I never heard from her again.

CHAPTER 5

L.S.M.F.T.

"I AM NOT a chain smoker," Gladys Blake, my loving mother, assured her sister Alice. "If you're a chain smoker, it means you light another cigarette with the one you're putting out. I always put mine out before I light another one," she said proudly. The Surgeon General would have been delighted. Alice was not much bigger than a cigarette. She was always sickly small and thin, but she kept up her end. Her Thin face looked like a road map to find an abusive husband. She never found a bad mate she didn't like. Her hair was styled like a flapper because it didn't take much to maintain it. The color was bland, between dark and light with some grey sprinkled in for highlights. Most abusers don't like their women looking too attractive. Might attract alternatives. Alice and my father both smoked Pall Malls. My mother preferred the unfiltered Lucky Strikes.

"L.S.M.F.T.," Gladys recited, showing Alice the letters on the pack of Lucky's she kept close at all times. Later I read that when people wake up in the middle of the night and the house is on fire, non-smokers grab family pictures and mementos to try to save them, and smokers always grab their cigarettes. "Do you know what that stands for," Gladys asked.

"No, but I'm sure you're gone tell me." Alice responded, knowing she really didn't care since it was not her brand anyway.

"Lucky Strike Means Fine Tobacco," Gladys said proudly. I was passing through the kitchen during this conversation, and since I couldn't find anything sharp to throw myself on, I decided to maybe go next door and use Granny's phone to call the MENSA people and see if they were aware of the fine tobacco situation. The phrase "think tank" always comes to mind when I remember that conversation. I liked Alice Crowe, my aunt. She was always nice to me and always had kind words for me, unlike Gladys.

Ian Fleming and Rod McKuen saved my life during the sixties. They were constant companions. Whenever things got too bad, I could always count on my two buddies to help me escape. "007 on Stanyon Street". Now that would have made a great story. I was always sure I could kill people as efficiently and coldly as James Bond, especially if they smelled like Lucky Strikes. My James Bond fantasy wasn't all cold hard killing, I had my sensitive side too. I learned how to love a woman without reservations from Rod McKuen, regardless of how much it would hurt later. Damn, you, Rod McKuen.

Am I being too hard on Gladys? Maybe. She grew up without parents from a young age and was bounced around from relative to relative. Her father shot her mother, then shot himself. Gladys contends it was an accident when he shot her mother and then was so distraught (a word she never used) that he shot himself. She, Alice and brothers Bud and Fess all grew up in the same situation, but, unlike Gladys, they were not mean and bitter. Life dealt them a shitty hand and they moved on. They loved their children and extended families. Gladys hated me mainly because I was smart, starting at an early age. I still wonder, why would you resent your child because he was smart? Using that same logic as our guideline, she adored Earl.

I was fourteen the last time she beat me. Mrs. Hayes, a real looker who had looked at my pop a time or three, showed up for her regular half-gallon purchase on Friday afternoon. Pop wasn't there, leaving only me to mind the store. I never hesitated. I took a half gallon from a hole in a barren cornfield and took it to her car. She paid me and I took the money in the house and put it on the table. The queen of Lucky Strikes had witnessed the entire transaction. For a woman only four feet eleven inches tall, she was pretty handywith a belt. Her weight helped, I'm sure.

She laid into beating me on the backside for selling the liquor to one of our best customers. Although her rage indicated she would have no son of hers selling liquor, I'm quite sure she was mad that I sold it to a woman as pretty as that. And probably she had seen Mrs. Hayes smiling at pop before. She was on fire with the belt and couldn't stop. Finally, the belt buckle hit me in the balls from behind and I went down. When I could breathe again and regained my legs, I grabbed her by the throat, slammed her against some exposed studs, and promised through gritted teeth "If you ever touch me again, you'd better kill me, because if you don't!" I can't say that our relationship became a filial, loving one after that, but we had reached a clear understanding.

"Pack some clothes," pop said a couple of weeks later. "We're going on vacation." This announcement sounded as suspect and alien as some of the things you only heard out of Roswell, New Mexico. Unbelievable. Oh, we had taken a vacation or two in the past, usually to the Cherokee Indian Reservation in Cherokee, North Carolina, but these were never spontaneous. They were planned well in advance and usually included an aunt and uncle or two and their kids. I hated Cherokee, not the Indians but the long hours cramped in a hot car, with my mother screaming all the way there and back. Windows up and the smell of fine tobacco burning the pristine tissues of my lungs. And we could never stop to pee unless she needed to pee.

"Where are we going?" I asked suspiciously.

"How 'bout Daytona Beach," pop declared proudly. And within an hour or two, we were on our way, six of us in an old black Chrysler New Yorker. My oldest sister Donna and her husband Albert were also going with us. We drove into Daytona Beach around three in the morning. The tide was out and the sky was clear. Enough moonlight to see small waves gently licking the white sand. I was suddenly glad we were there. You could drive on the beach in those days. Albert drove a couple of miles down the beach, pointing out the "no vacancy" signs on every motel.

"We'll just have to drive back a little ways and get a room that's not so close to the beach. Then we can drive back to the beach in the morning," he declared. We never stopped. He drove all the way back to Conyers and we never got our feet wet. We did stop at a Stuckey's to go to the bathroom on the trip back and Pop bought us a pecan log roll. They were sickly sweet. The house was still smoldering when we turned into the driveway. It was a total loss. Everything we owned (I thought), at least everything I owned, was gone. I later discovered some of our family albums filled with pictures had been stored in a pantry in my Granny's house. What luck, huh? My guess is they were tired of this house that was partially finished, or maybe more tired of the mortgage every month. Or maybe it was in the sightline of the Russians, and we needed to find a better place to build our bomb shelters. So, erasing my entire life was worth correcting that inconvenience. We miraculously were able to move into an apartment that very night. Pop already had the key to it. Later, when Albert was drinking heavily, he told me Uncle Fess had torched the house for fifty dollars.

CHAPTER 6
FOX 97.1

"Good Times and Great Oldies!"

I took some time off after Quixie to try to repair my fried circuits and wallow in self-pity. Radio is a powerful drug and I couldn't leave it alone. I think I've always had an addictive personality anyway, although I never did any drugs. I did try marijuana once and cocaine once. Both times there was a woman involved and I could never say no to a pretty woman. Neither of the highs that those drugs provided came close to radio though.

> **Production note:** *Please insert "This Old Heart of Mine" by the Isley Brothers. I was always off the page when I played this at Fox 97 (a firing offense), but it always made me feel good. (Off the page is when you play something that is not on the regular playlist.)*

Dennis Winslow was so nice, I was sure that if you cut him with a knife, he would bleed molasses. He had worked at WQXI FM (94Q) when I worked at WQXI AM (Quixie). He was program director at Fox 97. He smiled often and always acted like he was glad to see you. He was balding already but made up or it with a nice thick mustache that went well with his big smile and warm eyes that squinted every time he used that smile. He reminded me of a Boy Scout leader who wasn't a pedophile. He was happily married and had a small child.

"I need a job," I said flatly, no explanation required for someone who was a seasoned radio veteran. Radio is showbiz and no matter how good the show is, it always comes to an end, so radio people moved around a lot.

"OK," he agreed. "I'm gonna turn you over to Alan Sledge and he'll get you trained and work out a schedule for you. Do you know Alan?"

"Just from listening to him."

Alan was being groomed by Disney (the owner of Fox 97) for a program director job in the future. He was talented, but also looked good in a suit, very corporate. He liked young Asian boys. He had perfect dark hair, perfect teeth, was slim, and looked very professional. I didn't care that he was a fudge packer. He was always nice to me. I wound up doing his midday slot almost as much as him because he was always off somewhere learning all the Disney secrets, or on an all-inclusive fudge packer trip to Thailand or somewhere.

As we were getting a little older, the music of our past became even more important to us. The ancient Greeks had a saying "there's always a better time in the past." I liked the oldies, but the playlist was short, so you had to close your ears sometimes to avoid hating certain songs. The playlist primarily consisted of songs recorded between 1964 and 1969, the period often referred to as the second generation of Rock and Roll. At Quixie sometimes the music would make you crazy. We played the top 40 songs and there was about a one hour and forty-minute separation. That means a big hit was played over and over every one and a half to two hours.

"Cocooning" was how Dennis explained it to me. This was the entire premise of what was played on Fox 97. The music was appropriate for all family members. Cocooning was what people did when they decided to settle down and have kids. They created their own little worlds and wanted what was best for all the family. "It's okay to have a beer during the football game on Sunday," Dennis explained, "but moderation is key with our audience."

The phone rang on my second shift on the air a. She said, "you have a really nice voice."

"Alan's not here. I'm new. He should be back next week," I told her politely.

"I called to talk to you," she said. "My name is Angie."

"Do you work for the station, or…?"

"Let's just say I'm a friend of the station."

"Well, it's good to meet you, Angie, but I can't talk because I'm still trying to learn the ropes. I've already hung myself with them a couple of times today."

"We'll talk again soon," she promised. She sounded really good on the phone, so from previous experience, the ones who sound really good, usually don't look really good. I'm not saying they're all fat, but they are all fat. Now don't get me wrong, I have invested in a bag or two of flour in my lifetime. Any guy who says he hasn't is a liar. Morgan once told me, I go in and immediately hit on the fattest one there. They appreciate it. I take them out to the car and not only satisfy the demon but save a lot of money on buying expensive drinks for women who were never going to get naked with me anyway. When you're not that desperate, they don't feel the pressure and will screw up sometimes. Reminded me of a really fat bartender I knew once. She said I know I'm fat but at the end of the night, you would not believe the good-looking guys who want to screw me, and she always obliged. Excuse me while I go gut a hog just to get those images out of my mind.

> **PRODUCTION NOTE:** *How about some Temptations' "Ain't Too Proud to Beg."*

The Fox 97 Oldies Concert was coming up shortly. The Atlanta Falcons could never fill the Georgia Dome, but the oldies concerts always had it bursting at the seams. I would be on the air until about the start of the show, and my plan was to mosey on down with my all-access pass, hang out behind the stage, maybe eat something and people watch. "Good Times and Great Oldies" was exactly the right name for the show. Every person seemed to be having all the fun they wanted. The excitement was contagious.

"I'm Angie," the tall, thin brunette said, her green eyes sparkling. She had a great figure and her face was as pretty as a porcelain doll. She extended her hand. I never asked how she got a backstage pass.

"Do I know you? My memory is not that good these days. I think I would remember if we had met."

"We talked on the phone…the second day you were on the air," she reminded me.

I smiled and she said, "What's so funny?"

"Nothing," I confessed. "I just thought you were fat."

She looked herself up and down and said, "I have big boobs but I've never been called fat."

"Is your husband here? I'd like to meet him."

"He's home with the kids. This is my night out," she said proudly.

"Is your wife here tonight?" she quizzed.

"I don't have a wife, just a broken heart I'm trying to get over."

"Let me know if you need any help getting over her," she smiled again.

"You're married. I don't date married women," I lied.

"Too bad," she pouted. We walked out together that night for her security, not mine. "It was great to meet you finally," she seemed sincere. We came to my car first.

"Get in," I said quietly, and we headed to Riverbend. You never learn, do you? This time it would be different because I was sure that I could never fall in love with another woman again.

Angie Higgins started to dress and I asked what her husband was going to say. "Who cares. That's been over a long time. I love my two boys and it's easier to stay married than put them through hell." Déjà vu all over again, as Yogi always said.

"I can't see you again because you're married and it's too complicated," I proclaimed.

"Not your decision," she said flatly and I took her to her car.

"Goddamn it! Did you just mention the Gold Club on the air?!" Dennis demanded as he burst into the studio. I was doing afternoons that week. What happened to Mr. Nice Guy?

"Yeah. Big wreck on Piedmont. I said it was near the Gold Club." The Gold Club was the premier strip joint in Atlanta. Atlanta, being in the Bible Belt, was famous for its full nudity strip clubs. And these clubs had their biggest week when the Southern Baptist Convention was in town. Finally, a religion I could understand and embrace.

He was furious. "Don't ever mention something like that again. This is a family station!" As he left, I thought your fault, you hired me. Dear God, I stole a bus and he knew it and still hired me. But I apologized again later. I was determined to tow the line and keep my life and career in order.

Except for the Angie part. I really enjoyed that part being out of line and I wouldn't want it any other way. "I think I need a wife," I said after a couple of beers with Morgan. We were at TGI Fridays in the Prado, our new watering hole. Close to home and Fox 97.1.

"Every man needs a wife," Morgan said. "How else would you know how many beers you've had." We got a good laugh out of that. "What do you need with a wife? Get a dog if you're lonely. Or another beer."

"I'm not lonely, it's just that sometimes I think I need someone to come home to."

"Yeah, some cold bitch who won't even give you sloppy seconds." Morgan, the great philosopher. "Listen. Why are you still beating yourself up over this bitch? And don't even say she's not the reason. I'm glad she's gone. There are a million guys in this city who would swap places with you. Get over it! What did you think, she was gonna stay home and make a meatloaf or a green bean casserole and wait for you every night? If they didn't have that one little special part, there'd be a bounty on them. Except for that, why would you even talk to them?"

"Point taken, Morgan." He was right. We never talked that much, but we clawed a lot.

I'm sure the guy who invented cigarettes did so because he didn't want to talk after sex. "Listen, I'm going back to Pittsburg next month and see some of the guys I used to work with at KDKA. It's a dual celebration. My divorce will be final. I might even find me a Polish girl who likes accordion music while I'm there. Why don't you go with me?"

"I'm allergic to accordion music." When I was eight pop signed me up for accordion lessons with Mr. John Fox of the Fox Music Conservatory (which consisted of a rented dining hall in the basement of the Masonic Lodge in Covington every Tuesday and Thursday night). I lost interest after I mastered the accordion and Gladys would tell me in front of company to get my accordion out and play *"Amazing Grace."* Probably another mistake I made, giving up the accordion. I could have been a concert accordionist by now or at least been working weekends in a mariachi band.

"Tell you what though, when you get back, we'll tie one on and really celebrate your divorce. Is it okay if I call your wife while you're gone?"

"Be my guest," he laughed.

PRODUCTION NOTE: *Even though we did not play it on Fox 97, I would like to invoke some journalistic latitude and play ELO's "Evil Woman" here.*

"I just wanted you to be the first to know there's an

opening at WPLO, if you're tired of Oldies," Morgan said on the phone. I was glad he was back.

"Is Jean Raven still there?"

"Nah, she left. Married a dentist and has two kids. She came by the station a while back to visit and her ass looked like a Buick."

"What a loss. So, who's leaving PLO?"

"Me! I'm in Pittsburg. Going back to KDKA, not even working a notice. I was alwayshappy here. After I married that bitch and took her away from that little coal town, my life went south. You should come here."

For the second time in my life, my heart was truly broken. Who's gonna love me now?

"Suppose I could be here like this every day," Angie asked. "Would you like that?" She spent lots of time with me at Riverbend. The first sign they are about to start nesting is hampers. When they bring in hampers and start organizing, it's just a matter of time.

"No," I said frankly. "You're still married."

"Well, it looks like not for long. Charles has filed for divorce and I've talked to the boys. They know we're not happy. It'll be friendly and we'll have joint custody. I want you to meet them." She was already planning our new life together.

"I don't really like meatloaf that often," I said. She thought I was giving her instructions on how to be my new wife.

"I'll cook anything you want," she promised. She was a beautiful woman, especially lying naked in a dark room. Boz Scaggs was on the stereo singing *"Love, Look What You've Done to Me."* They are so soft and pretty but can cause so much pain. I knew I had to get ahead of the eminent pain or I'd be the one suffering.

Production note: *A little Boz here.*

I almost tried to call Elain in Los Angeles, but I fought the urge. (That's a lie. I called five times but didn't leave a message).

"If I never hear another oldie in my life, it will be too soon," I said to Linda Scarborough. I was sitting at Richard's Lounge in Decatur. She was the main bartender there and Hadley Young was her, what's the term "boyfriend, love interest, better half…?" He and I would become best friends for a long time. Linda loved all kinds of music, especially oldies, so I guess you could say we had a love-hate relationship. Linda had seen me in the parking lot a time or two with Angie. Angie didn't drink and was married, but at least didn't quote Bible verses to try to save my soul. Linda had seen many of my women throughout the years. She always withheld her opinions. Hadley was two years older than me and Linda was about five years older than him. She was a pretty woman with red hair and a hot trigger. Bad temper. Could hold a grudge forever. She scared me, so I tried to stay on her good side. We socialized through the years but I never tried to make her mine. Why taint a part of my life that was uncomplicated?

"She's pretty," Linda pointed out as I came back in after spending a few minutes outside with Angie.

"She is," I agreed.

"Is she the one?" She pressed.

"Yes, for right now," I admitted, not knowing that

soon I would eliminate her as thoroughly from my life as I did happiness a long time ago.

"Have you met Terri, our new bartender?" Linda introduced us.

"You're very pretty, Terri. Are you married?" She could pass for Madeline Stowe's twin sister. Dark eyes, dark hair, dark tan (healthy, not that store-bought yellow orange), dark red lipstick and probably a dark soul.

"Yes."

"Happily?" I pressed. She smiled.

PRODUCTION NOTE: *This would be a great time to play "Honky Tonk Women" by the Rolling Stones.*

CHAPTER 7

BENNY

"All I'm gone do is slick leg her," Benny said, his breathing labored. "I ain't gone hurt her." Charlie and I were in the barn with Benny and the thought that kept going through my mind was what Gladys always said, "He's not right."

I didn't know what he was talking about, but Charlie seemed to. Benny was over six feet tall, muscular, with thick, long brown hair. When you looked into his dark eyes, it was obvious nobody was driving the tractor. He always wore heavy, mud-stained work Boots and faded blue Oshkosh overalls with no shirt and probably no underwear either. He seemed to always have a hand stuck inside his overalls.

"I'm gone give y'all a dollar a piece just to get her in the barn. Y'all can pretend you playing hide 'n seek or something. Just don't let nobody come in here."

"Let's go, Charlie," I said. He hesitated and I went home. I wanted no part of Benny. I had known for a long time that his mental brakes did not work. I was unsure if he even had them like most people.

The object of his affection was Katrina Ledford, a seven-year-old with blonde, wavy hair, blue eyes and a perfect smile.

It was a typical early summer evening, with visiting relatives and neighbors sitting on the front porch, dipping, chewing, smoking, talking, and shelling peas or butter beans, depending on what was coming in. Katrina's mother often helped to earn a little extra money. Her husband was in jail and she struggled just to get by. My aunt and uncle tried to help her as much as possible, knowing first-hand the complications caused by the incarceration of a loved one.

I spent every Friday night at Charlie's house along with my brother, Gladys Jr., whose IQ could freeze a puddle on a hot summer day. We always watched "The Friday Night Frights," hosted by Bestoink Dooley (probably not his real name). He rotated weekly movies featuring Boris Karloff as The Mummy, Lon Chaney as The Wolfman, and Bela Lugosi as Count Dracula. There may have been others, but these were the scariest movies ever made, causing bad dreams that made your heart race all night long. Even though The Mummy dragged one foot, had one arm and hand wrapped tightly to his body, and barely moved with the other arm outstretched, he could always catch up to his prey and choke the life out of him with his one good hand. Boris Karloff was scary even when he wasn't dressed like The Mummy.

Lon Chaney seemed like a nice likable guy, although clearly troubled. And when the moon was full, the wolf inside him would emerge, chase you down, and rip you to pieces. He always seemed sincerely sorry the next day. Bela Lugosi was Dracula. I don't think he was acting. The accent, the dark eyes, and all that quickness spelled doom. When he wanted you, you were dead. His movies were the scariest; not a waste of celluloid, like when they made those Twilight movies. Bella is a woman who fools around with vampires and tries to understand them. There was nothing to understand about the other Bela; he just wanted to suck you dry as quickly as possible.

Benny was scarier than all of them. Charlie, Earl, and I were hiding under his bed one night which we did often just to eavesdrop. His sister Sarah came in not knowing he was in the room. He closed the door, unzipped his overalls, and exposed his uncircumcised penis to her. "Leave me alone or I'll call daddy," she said in that sweet southern drawl.

"I ain't gone hurt you this time Sarah. This ain't gone take but a minute." He was on her and had her on the bed, groveling and pulling her clothes off. She was crying and he had his big hand over her mouth, almost smothering her. I scampered out and hit him with a lamp, crumpling the plastic covered shade and shattering the bulb. She jumped up and ran and I was right behind her. She ran outside and didn't come back that night. Benny left and spent the night in the barn.

"Aunt Dessa, Benny was trying to hurt Sarah," I told her.

"They was just playing, hon. You need to go on home now. Uncle Tobe is on the way home and all you gone do is make him mad. Go on now." I never mentioned what happened to Sarah and she never brought it up to me either.

I learned later that Katrina had fallen in the barn and hurt herself. There was blood on the inside of her thigh, and her Fisher Price "Little People" panties were torn. Her mother kept trying to stop her crying, but she kept on, so they went home. The next day Charlie said, "You want to walk to the store and get a Pepsi and a Baby Ruth?" Mr. Sander's store was only about three miles away, a trip we made often.

"I don't have any money," I admitted.

"It's allright. I got two dollars," he said. I lost my taste for Pepsi's and Baby Ruth's that day. I just wanted to go home and be alone.

Before Uncle John died, Benny and he would sit on the porch, roll Prince Albert cigarettes, and talk about all the women who lived near us. Uncle John talked a lot about Sarah, so my guess is both "were not right." Crimes went unreported in those days and my family invented the notion of "need to know." They would rarely tell you anything, especially the truth.

Benny and Uncle John would sit and sip home brew made in a dark place under the house out of strained, rotting fruit, Charlie and I had discovered. The smell was strong and apparently, it was potent. They drank it every day after Benny's chores were done and up until it was time for aunt Dessa and Uncle Tobe to get home from work. They both became scarce then, with Uncle John sleeping it off in the back bedroom and Benny pretending to be working around the barn.

Even at a young age, I knew the shame and humiliation of being white trash. Whenever I was around other children and their families, whether at school, at church, or in town, I could tell they didn't live like we did. Nothing was ever normal in our family. Small disagreements could escalate quickly to the point of violence. I had seen two people shotunder those circumstances. They both survived, but instinctively I knew the rest of the world was not like this. Screaming, pouting, and making up after a couple of days was not within the realm of our existence. So, I escaped to the world of Ian Fleming, Rod McKuen, The World Book Encyclopedias and the Science Encyclopedias.

Nobody ever planned weddings or even engagements in those days. There was just the usual explanation of "She run off." And on sexual matters, you did not sleep with a girl or woman. "I went off with her," was enough explanation for the private matter. And the little talk about the birds and bees was explained by Gladys. "Them lil' ole gals will get you in trouble," she must have told me a thousand times. Yes, I hope so. Ah, the depths of the wisdom this woman possessed were bottomless. How could she not have found enough kindness in her heart to eat her young, I will never understand. She hated motherhood.

Apparently, there really is a God: Benny tripped over a hayfork and fell out of the upper level of the barn. No one was home at the time but him. It was speculated it might have taken several hours to die, lying there with a broken back, probably a concussion from the looks of his head and, lots of cleansing blood. Are you washed in the blood of the Lamb, you motherfucker? I was quite sure he begged for forgiveness in the time before his passing, his blood pooling under scattered hay and mule shit. At the end they all do that, regardless how bad they've been. I don't believe it's as simple as that. Live a horrible life and everything is forgiven right at the end. Hopefully, he's down near the fire, smoking his Prince Albert cigarette and the overseer is constantly screaming "What is that God Awful smell?!" I'm sure it wasn't Jesus who called Benny home. On the bright side, there was lots of fried chicken that week.

PRODUCTION NOTE: *"Homecoming," by Tom T. Hall.*

CHAPTER 8

WZGC, ATLANTA, Z93, CLASSIC ROCK N ROLL

"You know, Bob," all the signs are there. You live downtown, you're thirty-five years old, you have a thirty-two-inch waste and you've never been married. You're gay," I explained after a few Buds, not Bud Lights. Bob Bailey always said if you're gonna drink, drink. None of that sissy stuff.

"Ted Bundy was convicted on less evidence," Bailey admitted. "I'm not gay," he said, "but I'm pretty sure this guy I've been fucking is." It was always hard to get one over on Bailey. Bailey did afternoons 3pm to 7pm on Z93. Tony Hayes fired Steve Maple who did 7pm to midnight because he caught him off the page and playing *"Fat Bottom Girls."* I was rarely on the page from then on. I loved Tony Hayes. He let me get away with murder, but it paid off. The night show was a rolling carnival that just happened to play some good songs occasionally. I was in my element— out of control and happy. I was finally over Elain. I'm lying. I tend to do that in my fantasy world.

> **Production note:** *Please play "Waiting on a Friend" by the Stones. Not on the page, but I liked it and played it often.*

Linda Scarborough was working at a place called Bud's Eastside, so this became my new watering hole. Bud was a total nutjob, but his food was good and lots of pretty women hung out there. It was a lot like the Cheers bar, except at Cheers, they all had teeth. Bud had a habit of not wearing his bottom partial plate, exposing lots of gum on the bottom in the middle. He also had a habit of marrying younger women who always ended up taking him to the cleaners. Ain't love grand? He was a hard worker and ran a successful place, so I guess he was entitled. The only thing he loved more than younger women was Kentucky basketball.

I was finally in love with a woman named Melanie Hall. She was gorgeous, smart, and of course, married. But this one was different. She had filed and we had talked seriously about getting married immediately after that. I was ready for the meatloaf and casserole although I didn't even know if she could cook. I kept looking for flaws in her pretty oval face, her perfect body, her attitude, and demeanor, but I always came up short. The only fault she had was me. This was the real deal. Five eight, blonde, blue eyes, a good talker and a great kisser, with full soft lips. Her teeth were perfect and she had a lot of them (remember, we were at Bud's, teeth optional).

Mel had never been to Key West; I had been there once and loved it. I used to do live shows on Z93 from a bar named Hemingway's in Decatur every Friday night. I'm not sure if there was any affiliation, but there was also a Hemingway's in Key West on themain strip just across the street from a really fancy Holiday Inn where I had stayed with a dark-haired woman. Can't remember her name. Every afternoon we would sit at Hemingway's for happy hour. Late the first day we noticed everyone was getting up,

drinks in hand, and walking down the street toward the ocean. I asked a stranger what was going on and he said "Just bring your beers and follow the crowd. You'll see."

Every afternoon at the very end of the United States, everyone would walk to the ocean and watch the sunset. It was spectacular and peaceful. When I described all this to Mel, we decided this would be the perfect place for a honeymoon. We could eat, drink, fish, love and start over at the end of our known world. Maybe even throw beer bottles at Cuba.

> **PRODUCTION NOTE:** *Please insert Bertie Higgins' "Key Largo" here. And if you're a twenty-five-year-old production assistant who wears a fedora, this is not negotiable. No substitution allowed!*

Big Bear was my unofficial producer at Z93. He had a wicked sense of humor (I wondered how he got so bitter at the age of twenty-four) and desperately wanted to be a radio star. Most of the really funny guys are big and fat. Bear was no exception. He helped with writing the show and doing on-air bits. He brought a younger edge to the show so we were able to appeal to a larger audience. Every afternoon we would spend some time going through the news and deciding which way we were headed that night. "Nothing going on. Shitty news day," Bear complained. (I'm not sure I ever knew his real name). "Here's a big one. Six people showed up in Avondale to protest cutting down an old oak tree to build a shopping center or something."

"That's it!" I declared. "A lost cause. If that doesn't describe this show, then nothing does." Bear shook his head and started jotting down ideas, always able to make something out of nothing, and make it funny. We announced at the beginning of the show that the protest was much more important than it appeared. Captain Rhett Butler is actually buried under that tree and that's the part they were trying to keep quiet. Let the protests begin!

With his voice electronically distorted, a foreman for the construction company (Bear's clever disguise) called in and said he'd get fired if this got out, but they were planning to move Captain Butler's body to Oakland Cemetery where lots of other famous people were buried. He had no known relatives here since he was originally from Charleston, so they didn't expect any legal problems. The phone lines were flooded, even more so than the nights when we had the psychic on (who survived mostly on alcohol and nicotine, by her own admission).

The county offices were attacked the next day by angry people who could not believe the insensitivity and planned violation of Captain Butler's final resting place. Even though the newspaper ran a couple of articles that clearly explained that Captain Rhett Butler was a fictional character in *"Gone with The Wind,"* the protests raged for a week. It was good to see that there were lots of people still out there who cared about doing the right thing. And a little scary, too.

"Just say yes and I will be on a plane today," Elain promised.

"I thought you were happy in Los Angeles," I said. I had called to tell her I was getting married. I felt I had to or I would never be able to move forward.

"Don't do this to me," she said, starting to cry. "This can't be happening."

"Look, it just was not meant to be. Can you at least be happy for me?"

"No." She was honest. "Don't do this, baby. Please don't. I'll do anything you ask, just don't do this."

"I have to. I want a chance to be happy. I didn't want you to hear this from anyone else. I have to move on," I explained gently.

"You can never move on and neither can I. You know that." She was crying.

"I gotta go," I said. She hung up. Funny. I was getting better. I didn't feel like killing myself for about ten minutes. A new record.

PRODUCTION NOTE: *"Take My Breath Away," by Berlin.*

Mel and I were married at the Dekalb County courthouse at noon on a Thursday. I offered several times to let her off the hook, be she politely declined, knowing that I was the one who was nervous. She never offered to let me off the hook and I'm thankful for that. We boarded a Delta flight to Key West just after five o'clock that day. Damned! Poor planning. We were going to miss the sunset. "What were we going to do?" I fretted. She pinched me hard on the arm.

"I don't think I can have children," she said on the plane. "We never discussed this...."

"You have me, so you don't need other children. I can be pretty childish," I joked. She wanted to be serious.

"Look, I love you. If we have children, great, if not I will always have you and you will always have me.

Pretty soon you can change my diapers to satisfy your motherly instinct." She pinched me again.

We had our wedding night dinner at Hemingway's. I don't remember what we ate. I was too focused on this wonderful woman. I do remember one thing about the restaurant, reading about Hemingway cats that have six toes. How creepy is that. Naming a freak after a man who once said, "The best thing in the world is making love to a beautiful woman." I couldn't wait to get Mel's clothes off, just to make sure she didn't have six toes. That could be a deal breaker, I pointed out, and got kicked this time."

"You know, I understand why you're not wearing a white dress on our wedding night, but did you have to go in the total opposite direction? "I asked. "I mean the black dress with the skinny straps is too tight, too short and shows too much of your breasts and long, creamy legs. You're a married woman now, you know," I pointed out.

"I want every man in this place to know how lucky you are," she said. "Maybe then you won't forget it!" I loved that smile.

We didn't stay too late or drink too much. We held hands and walked back to the Holiday Inn. The night was perfect with a slight ocean breeze. I was happier than I had been in a long time. And the best part was, she was not going to get up in the middle of the night and leave me to go home to someone else. She was all mine.

"I can't believe I'm fishing on my honeymoon," she complained. "And you even made me bait my own hook."

"I've missed this for a long time, "I admitted. "Having a bitching woman around constantly." We had rented a boat and tackle with no intention of catching any fish. We just followed some other boats out who seemed to know where they were going. We got plenty of sun and I could tell by the way she was smiling she was enjoying the day and her new life. And I was enjoying mine. A new wife, a new job and a happy future.

We had no schedule, just sat on the beach, tried new restaurants, took long walks and spent lots of time in our room. The trip was nearly over but our honeymoon was just beginning. I promised myself to never let it end.

PRODUCTION NOTE: *"One Love" by U2 would be perfect here.*

I have always been an early riser. I love drinking coffee and reading the paper in the morning. That's why I love the Waffle House. Always open and they had to take me in, as long as I was wearing shoes and a shirt. My new bride was sleeping soundly when I left the bed. I decided I would bring her breakfast when I came back. It was our last day in paradise. One more large calorie intake, one more long walk and one more sunset before we started our new life as an old married couple. I couldn't wait. "Cheese Danish, fruit and coffee for you, my highness." She was still sleeping, but now in a fetal position. She moved slightly, so I set her breakfast down and walked to the bed.

"She's gone. I'm sorry," the medic said. "Probably heart failure, but we won't know for sure until…."

She was thirty and had pinched me every time I reminded her she was over the hill. I drifted in and out of reality, certain that this was just another crazy dream I had conjured up in my on-going fantasy world life. I was lost. I stayed a few more days in Key West, never seeing the sunset, but I saw it rise every day just like everything was normal.

Her mother and father came down immediately after I called them. I should have been taking care of them during this time of sorrow, but they ended up taking care of me. At the end of the fourth day, during a beautiful sunset, we walked to the ocean and scattered her ashes and what was left of my life into the Gulf of Mexico.

Production note: *"She's Gone," by Hall and Oates.*

It was late when I arrived in Atlanta, raining and windy. I went straight to the radio station on Johnson Ferry Road in North Atlanta and slipped a handwritten note under the general manager's door. "I won't be back. R."

Who's gonna love me now?

*

View from the gurney: one-story brick building; all the windows were frosted so you couldn't see in or out. Not sure if they were trying to keep me from seeing out or someone from seeing in. Neat landscaping. Locks everywhere. Can't pass through a single door without someone clicking you through. As usual with any healthcare facility, all healthcare providers are overweight, some grossly so. And all their uniforms looked like they were washed in hot and dried on high, the same look I saw many times on people wearing T-shirts at NASCAR races. I always wash on cold and dry on low. It seemed important for me to express a cognizant thought for some reason. Wash whites separately, I remembered.

"Mr. Blake. Mr. Blake," she pressed. She was snapping her fingers at me. How rude! She was young, maybe thirty and black, real black, National Geographic black. No bone in her nose as far as I could see. Long, shoulder length hair. Indian hair probably. Morgan always told me if it looks anything like real hair on them, it's fake. He also told me anytime a white guy admitted to fucking a black girl, he always said "she looked just like Jayne Kennedy." He was right, I confessed. This one had nice white teeth and big eyes, but she was a little plump. She looked nothing like Jayne Kennedy, so obviously I had not fucked her. I think she said her name was Christy something. "Mr. Blake," she pressed. "What do you remember? Do you know where you are?" Nag, nag, nag.

"I was skinny dipping," I admitted. The drugs they had given me still felt good. I would like to have a mason jar full of that to take home with me. Half gallon, please. You don't have to charter it just for me.

"You're not making sense. Skinny dipping where?" She sounded like she thought I was crazy. The nerve of this woman! Just because I'm in a nuthouse....

"I was skinny dipping in the River Styx. I didn't have any coins on my eyes to pay the ferryman, so they brought me here, south of Hell."

"Do you know where you are now?" She pressed.

"Did Elain call?" I asked softly. "When she does, make

sure you come and get me." I went back to try to talk the ferryman into taking me over.

'Here' was Southwood, a secure place in Riverdale, Georgia where they take nutjobs and substance abusers. Entrance was granted to me immediately because I scored high in all categories. I wondered if I were to graduate, would that be as high an honor as getting your GED? Off white. That's all I remember. Walls, furniture, clothing, ceiling, thoughts…and that nasty clean smell of antiseptic products. "Mr. Clean gets rid of dirt and grime and grease in just a minute…." Not sure why I remembered that. I had casually mentioned to my meddling son, I might end it all. I'm sure I probably meant with Elain. He panicked and called the cops. They took me to Rockdale Hospital and then Southwoods graciously agreed to accept me once they verified my insurance. So, they strapped me to a gurney, filled my veins with something that sounded like Rimron or maybe rim job, but it was a pleasant experience anyway.

"Can I borrow a couple of quarters," I asked, knowing half dollar pieces were rarely carried by people anymore.

"There are no vending machines here," she explained. For a smart woman with lots of degrees, she was not too smart. The ferryman will not give you a ride without coins.

Group Therapy, 10:00 am Tuesday. Star date… never mind.

The rim job/Rimron left a terrible dope over. Trouble swimming back to the surface. I was ushered into a room with fifteen chairs. I always counted, just like when I'm driving down the interstate, I always count the number of wheels on the eighteen-wheelers just to make sure. You can't trust anybody these days. (To date no one has cheated. They all have exactly eighteen, I am happy to report.) There were about eight of us plus another person who had a counselor's degree or was just available to guide this three-hour tour, no wait that was the captain's job on Gilligan's Island. She gave directions about seating in some Jamaican-type accent, but I winked at her, knowing the accent was from some darker continent that didn't advertise all inclusive vacations to couples. But, then again, this was all inclusive....

Robin (no last names allowed) was seated on my right as I shuffled in. He was probably in his early fifties, with shoulder length brown hair, somewhat wavy. He had no gray hair, so obviously not washing it for weeks at a time kept away the gray. (Note to self: stop washing hair if you want to continue looking young). He wore wire rimmed round glasses and had a Buffalo Bill Cody/John Lennon looking mustache with a soul patch. Like the rest of us he had that "I'm wearing the clothes I was brought in with look." "You know, if they were to drape a skanky looking Chinese woman over you with her hand in your wallet pocket, you'd look just like John Lennon before he was allergic to shampoo," I pointed out, just trying to make friendly conversation.

"Fuck you, nutball," he replied in a welcoming way. Some people just don't warm up to strangers right away. After we were all seated and had avoided making any eye contact with each other, the counselor took over.

"Today, we will start by introducing ourselves, give a brief history of your life, and tell us why you are here."

"Do you mind if I ask what your credentials are?" I asked.

She paused slightly and said "I'm not wearing a plastic band with my name on it around my wrist. Those are my credentials." I was starting to like her. "This is where we start to reconnect with each other," she droned, having made this speech on many previous Tuesdays. How could I reconnect with people I've never met? "Robin, we'll start with you."

He removed his glasses, slowly cleaned them with the underside of his shirt, exhaled and finally put his glasses back on. He blinked a few times, then started to speak. "There are some areas in this country where they don't care if you smoke weed or not. That's where I've spent my life the last few years. Eventually they're gonna make it legal. There's a time machine in Montauk, Long Island, and when I get out of here, I'm heading that way. Once I know exactly when it will be legal, I can make plans for the future then," he said sincerely. Moving right along. I assumed she had heard this story a few times.

"Mr. Cruz, you're next, I mean Manny," she said, realizing she had used his last name. She probably blushed, but you couldn't tell.

"Me? I haff no story. I here since 1962 and I make floors," he said in his best Frito the Bandito accent, like he was pulled out of the river last night. He was a rotund (fat) older man with some graying hair, wearing thick glasses. His jowls were unshaven. He used a cane for walking and in place of a comforting blanket, clinching it tightly all the time when he was not hobbling along. He had that Social Security walk. I had seen it many times. People develop it when they are trying to get Social Security Disability.

"So, I'm assuming since you've been here over thirty

years, they don't use grammar books as flotation devices," I pointed out, "or to even wipe your ass. Oh, that's right, you guys don't wipe your asses like we do. Why don't you learn the language, asshole?" I needed to take it out on somebody.

"I no...neffer mind. Your mother is a fucker, you."

"Mr. Cruz, we will not use that language here, I mean Manny," Don't get me started on her accent. "Mr. Blake, please refrain from antagonizing other people."

"Just trying to reconnect," I defended myself.

"Amy, tell us a why you're here, and a little about yourself." She looked clean and kempt, a new arrival, so the counselor didn't know anything about her. Amy was between plain and pretty. Her face looked like it had not totally formed enough to be pretty. Hard to describe. She had hair down to her waste, light brown and straight, clean and combed. She looked about nineteen. She had not been here long enough to perfect that who gives a fuck look. "I am from Ludowici, Georgia, and my best friend when I was growing up was Lulu Bobo from TyTy, Georgia." She giggled. "I always tell that story. It's true." No one else laughed. "I am not a drunkard and I have never used drugs except Bayer aspirin and Pamprin, but they are both legal. I am not here for any mental problems. I am here because I am an artist and if you have ever been around any artists, you know they are always misunderstood." She smiled uncomfortably when no one agreed openly with her summation. "I have something stuck in my head and can't get it out, no matter what I try." She started whistling the theme to the Andy Griffith show, the entire tune. Finally, Christy raised her hand palm out to end the concert. "I'm a whistler and that's the first song I learned to whistle. My mama would only let me watch certain shows on TV when I was little and on Nick at Night, they always showed the old Andy Griffith shows. I would practice the tune all the time. Finally, they wouldn't let me come back to school because I couldn't control my whistling. I would break out during the class and disrupt everything." She started whistling the same tune again, for emphasis, I suppose.

"That's enough for right now, Amy," the counselor interrupted.

"My mama sent me here to hopefully learn some new tunes," Amy said. Whistler's mother sent her here, I privately joked to myself.

PRODUCTION NOTE: *We need more padding in the group room.*

"Larry, you are next. Tell us a little something about yourself and why you're here," she pushed forward, hoping there might be a normal light at the end of this dark tunnel. Larry was about sixty-five, bearded, probably no hair since he wore a Georgia Bulldogs cap, red with a white Green Bay "G" on the front. Bald guys wear hats and nobody ever has a clue they're bald. He looked frail, short, and small. He started blubbering immediately about drinking a half gallon a day, children dying and wanting to see his grandkids graduate or at least grow up enough to drink a half gallon a day. We moved on while he was still sobbing.

"Susan, why don't you tell us a little about yourself and why you're here," the counselor pressed (I think her name was Christy or Kreeesty as she pronounced it). Susan said "you know" about six hundred times in a three-minute conversation. I finally ascertained she had a fondness for the sauce as well as Larry (and his grandkids, one and seven years old). She was pudgy, maybe forty-five, with a pageboy haircut, big nose, yellow teeth and pig eyes. She was not one of those girls who got prettier at closing time.

"Booze and lies, that's the story of my life," she said. I thought she was talking about me. "I have been a party girl all my life. I've worked but my parents have lots of money and they're always giving me big chunks on a regular basis. I had the means and the lack of will power, so here I am." Chunks of money. She's getting prettier. Must be close to closing time.

"Mr. Blake, I mean, Randy, tell us a little about yourself and why you're here."

"I'm expecting a phone call," I lied and walked out.

PRODUCTION NOTE: *Please insert "Hold on Loosley" by 38 Special.*

Robin confided in me the next morning at breakfast "I've been in these places fourteen times through the years. It's a roof over your head and three squares a day. It's a nice break from living in the van. And you rarely get cornholed unless you want to. Not like prison where you get it regular. Guys go in thinking it'll never happen to me, then next thing you know, five or six guys hold you down and go at it. All you can do is just enjoy the ride and hope nobody in line wants seconds, 'cause everybody knows the second time always takes longer." He smiled.

"Thanks for the advice, I think." Check, please!

"All I'm saying is if you want to get out, you got to

play the game. I want to stay in for a while and let the state pick up the tab, so I play the game," he admitted proudly. I sobered up quickly and the dope over passed. I was determined to become the model citizen if that's what it took to get out. Robin explained I was in on a ten thirteen which meant they could hold me as long as they deemed me a threat to myself or somebody else. How he came by this private information, I still don't know. Oh, that's right…time machine.

Group Therapy, 10am Wednesday "Mary, why don't we start with you this morning," the counselor began. Mary was tall, shapely, thin, pretty, if you like women without makeup, clear brown eyes, nice teeth and a sweet smile. She looked like the normal girl next door.

"Thank you and thank you to my Lord and Savior Jesus Christ. I am an alcoholic. I want to tell you first about when I became a Christian. I was five years old and fell and the breath was knocked out of me. I stopped breathing. They were giving me mouth to mouth and I could see myself walking around my body and I knew Jesus was on his way to get me. I saw Jesus that day. He don't look nothing like you think. Kinda scary really, not this friendly looking type with long hair. He is all business. But I could tell he loved me. And remember all those kids they said Wayne Williams killed? Well, he didn't because they were all killed at my house, by relatives of mine. I seen it all."

"Okay, let's move on," Christy interrupted, embarrassed. I was disappointed. Her story was starting to get interesting. "Mary, we can only discuss your story here, not speculation about someone else."

"It's not speculation," Mary said impatiently. "I seen it all. Them poor little children, and Wayne didn't do it. I am going to get him out. He is falsely imprisoned," she rattled on. I wondered if Wayne were working to get her out so she could get him out. I wouldn't mind cornholing Mary, I thought. Something attractive about a woman crazier than me. She reminded me of a man named Pinky I knew as a child. He was obsessed with Jesus too. He would look up and over his left or right shoulder and say things like "Can you believe what he just said?" We always called that "talking to Jesus." When you did it, most people left you alone. And by the way, I was sure he would have cornholed Jesus, given the opportunity.

"Rosa, you're next," Christy said pleasantly.

"Don't want to," Rosa replied under her breath. No one knew how long she'd been here, but it had been over a year. She wore the same pink sweat suit every day. She was a medium sized black woman with graying, natural hair and gargantuan tits that hung way down. One hung down several inches lower than the other. Larry once told me she draws over three thousand dollars a month, so she ought to get out and get a place of her own.

"Okay, then. How about you, Fulton," the counselor moved on cheerfully. Fulton had never met a crack pipe he didn't like. Bad crack. Wasn't that what got Len Bias and Magic Johnson? He was black, six feet tall and weighed maybe a hundred pounds. When he talked, it just sounded like mumbling. I think he said he was from Chicago and his hobby was partying. He was sickly thin and had the shakes, and his eyes had a pleading look, the whites yellowed with bulging red veins. If he lost another pound or two, Sally Struthers would probably cry and try to raise money for him. He kept on mumbling quietly.

"Thank you, Fulton," the counselor chirped. "Mr. Wallace, are you capable of sharing with us today?"

Few moments of strained silence. He finally looked up slowly.

"Is everything I say to you and the group confidential?" He asked. "'Cause I ain't going back to the big house again."

"Yes, as usual," she assured him.

"The part I hated about my work was they always offered you sex, sometimes money, but always sex. They would do anything I wanted if I didn't kill them. That was my downfall. I am a weak man. I could never turn it down. I only took contracts from husbands to kill their wives. I always got all the money up front, or no deal. And once I accepted the contract, whatever I did extra, besides just killing them, was a bonus. It's easier to kill women, easier to subdue them if things get out of hand. Sometimes if you're trying to kill a guy, he can turn the table on you. Then you're the one offering sex or money to save your ass." Robin told me later that Jerry Wallace was a tax accountant who had a sideline of stealing identities from tax returns and ordering credit cards to support his lavish lifestyle: breakfast and lunch at McDonald's and a cold can of SpaghettiOs for dinner. He speculated Jerry's only sex partner had been himself, willing or unwilling, possibly forcing himself on himself.

He was a little man with a really bad comb over. The strands were combed over from just above his left ear to just above his right ear. Thin, stringy hairs that did little to hide his baldness, only his insecurity. He wore Buddy Holly type glasses, with thick black frames. His eyes seemed to dart back and forth constantly. His clothes were baggy and out of style, unless plaid pants are still in. His face was small and pointed, and he tried to sneer when he talked, exposing gapped teeth, yellowing. The sneer was to emphasize the fact that he was a cold-blooded killer, I suppose. He had most of the money still available when he was captured. He did thirteen months in a minimum-security federal prison for tax fraud and identity theft. Somehow, they never charged him for all the murders. No bodies, and no women were reported missing. He also had to repay the thirty thousand dollars he had filched. He had become interested in murder mysteries about contract killers while he worked in the prison library. He had served more time in Southwoods than in the Federal Pen off Boulevard Avenue in Atlanta. Robin shared this information with me.

"How'd you kill them?" I had to know.

He wagged his right index finger back and forth and said, "No details, my friend. That'll get you every time. Let's just say they died with a smile on their faces."

The next three ring act was named Rada, pronounced Rayda, or just fruitcake for those of you familiar with Claxton, Georgia, where they make fruitcakes. I could tell the counselor was hesitant to call on her, so I couldn't wait to hear her story. "Rada, would you like to join in today?" She finally asked, nervously.

Rada nodded affirmatively and cleared her throat. She interlocked her fingers and touched them to her lips, pondering where to start. Or maybe to pray for Wayne

Williams. "My name is Rada and I'm not sure how long I've been here this time, but it's been a long time. I come here at least once a year, every time I come close to having… relations," she forced herself to say with her eyes turned downward. She was maybe forty, thin because nobody got fat in here, (a dollar twenty per meal is what they allotted for each meal per person, as Robin had told me), long hair, obviously a natural blonde because if she didn't even take time to brush her hair, I can't imagine her taking the time to bleach it. She never looked up much so I wasn't sure about the color of her eyes, but her lips looked like they hadn't been used to smile much. No smile lines.

"You mean sex, don't you?' the counselor chimed in cheerfully.

"Yes, but I don't like that word. It sounds nasty. It is nasty. I've seen mama have to wipe daddy off…." She shuddered and shook her head side to side and finally moved on. "Well, I come here at least once a year, because I am afraid of splinters," she said, waiting for us to shudder, I guess. "Whenever my mama and daddy would have, you know, relations… that night mama would wash out the rubber…I know they call them condoms now. I do know things, but we always called them rubbers. Well, mama would wash it out to save money and stick it on a broom handle on the porch to dry. I know that old broom handle had splinters, so no way do I want to get splinters in me." She closed her eyes and grimaced. Made me feel like grimacing too.

"Thank you, Rada. Mr. Blake. Would you like to share with us today?" I waited until all the laughter ended; a few snickers continued the whole session.

"I'd be happy to," I lied. "I was born here, and recently lost my wife. I don't normally drink alcohol, but her death ripped me apart. Next thing I knew, I was feeling suicidal. I would like to thank all of you for your kindness. I just want to get back on my feet as soon as possible and move on with my life." Teacher's pet. So now my plan is to take my newly found fear of splinters and get as far away as quickly as possible. The counselor nodded in agreement and appreciation. Scary. I sounded like the sanest one there.

Time for lunch. Taco salads. Robin always knew what was on the menu. The diabetic patients, the patients with high cholesterol, the patients with heart conditions or high blood pressure, and the ones on a low sodium diet all received the same food, three times a day, even though the meal tickets specified their diet requirements. At two grand a day per patient, you can't expect chef-catered meals.

Dr. Chandora, fourth session. (He's a shrink).

"You have made remarkable strides. Quite frankly, I thought you'd be with us for at least thirty days, given your history and the tragedy you've suffered." He was Indian, of course (not the Tonto type), and I wondered if all doctors in India were Americans. And who's running the store while he's here? He had thick glasses, thick black hair, a thick body and a thick accent. His clothes always looked brand new and expensive. Business was good. "I am going to release you tomorrow. I want you to continue the medications we have been giving you (you know, the ones that make the zombies laugh at how out of it you are) and I want to see you once a week until further notice" (or until the insurance maxes out, I understood). I also am going to suggest several support groups you should try and I want you to go to an AA meeting every week. You can pick one that is close to you and see if it fits."

"Thank you, doctor. I will do anything I can to get my life back on track as soon as I can. I want to get better." I never saw him again, or the support groups or the AA people. Or Jesus. By dark the next day, I was drunk and trying to call Elain.

PRODUCTION NOTE: *"Operator" by Jim Croce.*

CHAPTER 9

LARRY

Larry Brown's family was as poor as mine. The big difference was they all seemed to like each other. Mr. Brown and Mrs. Brown were always smiling and engaging their six sons. He worked as a mechanic and she stayed home, making sure her boys were properly raised. I always loved visiting them. It seemed like a real home. I had known Larry since elementary school. He was smarter than I was and had a quicker wit. We spent as much time together as possible. I would even drive my Honda 50 cc motorcycle to his house (seven or eight miles away) well before I had a driver's license. The cops didn't care about things like that then. They had other more important things to worry about, like repeat offenders who distributed moonshine.

My pop and Gladys both worked at the Bibb Manufacturing Company in Porterdale in Newton County. I was born in that mill town in the Porterdale Hospital. Dr. Mitchell delivered me and provided medical attention for all the employees of the Bibb. He also removed more tonsils and appendectomies, which were his most profitable procedures. Nobody questioned his judgment. The procedures were all covered by the Bibb insurance. And Dr. Mitchell had to make a living.

The old mill was a two-story brick structure with a basement built on the Yellow River in the middle of Porterdale. People worked there their entire lives and many of their children worked there after them. There weren't many jobs around in those days unless you could farm or pick cotton. Everyone lived in a mill house in Porterdale, with supervisors getting homes that often had three bedrooms, but most of them had two bedrooms and regardless of how large your family was, nobody complained about being crowded. And I guess if you never knew about something, you could not really miss it. Imagine trying to live without air conditioning now.

My father was still a night supervisor there the summer Larry and I had both turned sixteen. We were living in Conyers by then. We had a plan. Work all summer at the Bibb, save our money, and spend a week in Daytona Beach before school started back. (Hopefully get into trouble with some lil' ole gals). My father obliged us by getting us jobs on the night shift, eleven pm until seven am. The mill made all kinds of cord. Gladys ran a winder that tightly wrapped the strands of various materials to make nylon, cotton and blends of cord. I know it was a hard production job, but according to her, she worked harder than anyone else in the world. Probably even harder than the little kids at factories around the world. The difference was they weren't allowed to complain or smoke Lucky Strikes at every break. It was dirty and hard work and often I fell asleep in the bathtub in the morning, always too dirty to go to bed before I was clean. Women aged quickly at the Bibb and men just seemed to dry up, with all the juices of life slowly sucked out of them.

Most of the people at the Bibb were like the walking dead, called "lintheads' for the debris in their hair after work. They went to work, put in their hours and then went home. The largest thrill in Porterdale was at Christmas when every mill employee and each of their family members attended a party in the gym, decorated brightly and sporting a large tree. Stacked around the tree were fruit boxes, about one and a half times larger than a shoe box, filled with oranges, apples, a bag of mixed nuts and a bag of hard candy. Everybody who attended got one.

> **PRODUCTION NOTE:** *Please play Dolly Parton's "Hard Candy Christmas" here. I always think of the Bibb whenever I hear that song.*

Larry and I (and almost Earl) found a lake across the Irwin Bridge Road (maybe Irvin, still not sure) down an overgrown road to an old house that was completely rotted down. Earl fell in a creek and got wet and started crying, even harder after we laughed at him. He did a one eighty to "go tell Mama." The lake was maybe five acres large and loaded with bass. We fished there often; and swam there. It was deep and clean, the perfect spot to while away steamy summer afternoons. Larry couldn't swim but we had several well-patched inner tubes as our personal flotation devices. (Cars used to have tubes in their tires before tubeless tires were invented.)

Larry's father had refurbished a 1962 Ford Galaxy

two-door for his sixteenth birthday, black with a big engine and black rolled and pleated interior. I got a 1964 MGB from my sister who could no longer afford the repair bills or the $50 per month payment. So, we had wheels and ideas. I worked at a full-service gas station to make the payment and learn how to work on cars. Everything was less complicated then. Now the audio system manual in new cars is larger than the owner's manual in old cars. Go figure.

We went most places in Larry's carbecause it was so much bigger. Mine was a two-seater and would not hold an adequate number of "'lil ole gals," in case we were lucky enough to happen upon any. The year was 1968, the year of our sixteenth summer when Larry died. He had decided to go swimming alone. I was off and nobody knew where I was, so he even invited my brother to go, but he declined. I guess Earl wasn't so bad at this point in time after he learned to lie and keep secrets and stopped wearing white calypso pants with a striped shirt and rope belt identical to mine. Larry's parents started calling our house after dark that night, frantic because he had not come home. The next morning his car was found on the dirt road leading to our lake. Volunteers dug a hole in the dam to lower the water and started using drag hooks all around. Two inner tubes drifted quietly during all this commotion. I was standing on the dam when a hook caught Larry and brought him to the surface, face first. I will never forget the look of fright on his face. He had apparently fallen off a tube and panicked. Later, I guess as a tribute to Larry, my cousin Edward finished draining the lake and took all the fish to stock his own pond up the road. I still think about Larry over forty years later. If only I had been there when he called and wanted to go swimming.

"I'm fine," I kept assuring every adult who attended the funeral. My mother didn't go, but just about everybody else in the county did and of course everyone from our high school attended. More white trash trauma. Since it happened during the summer, after school began nobody ever mentioned Larry again. People move on and block out unpleasant memories, but I certainly did not. High school never prepares you for the real world or even reality. If instead of geometry they had taught Larry how to swim, he'd still be here. I am not blaming the school, only making a point: Most stuff you're taught is useless in the real world. But at that age the most important things were pep rallies, football games and Clearasil.

I didn't blame those who moved on and dealt with the shock of losing Larry. I blamed God. Why was Larry on his list? A young, promising, good person with a bright future ahead. How many times have you heard "oh he (or she) will get his (or hers) one day?" But they never do. The good do die young and the bad ones seem to live forever. And this is God's plan?

Some people deal with grief quietly and curse God quietly; some people grieve openly and curse God loudly; and then there was D.C. My father told this story and I could usually believe him, except for once when I was three or four and a rabid dog came around and he had to shoot it. He explained to me that there was no cure if you were bitten by a rabid dog. All they could do was tie you to the bed and shoot you between the eyes. He was great at bedtime stories.

On the first of the new year in 1953 D.C. lost someone close to him. He had learned to play the guitar a little and sat around for days, smoking, drinking and playing *"I'm So Lonesome I Could Cry"* over and over and over. Everybody thought they might have to send him to Milledgeville (that's where they sent all the crazy people in those days, if they didn't just tie them to a bed and shoot them between the eyes). Everybody pleaded with D.C. to get a hold of himself, but he just fell deeper into depression and played that song over and over in his bedroom. "It's like I knowed him all my life," D.C. whimpered. Later I discovered he had never even met Hank Williams, but apparently he felt close to him. I could imagine that Gladys might have reacted as severely if she had lost her pack of Luckies.

> **PRODUCTION NOTE:** *Do I have to tell you everything? You know what to play here.*

I never met Hank Williams either, but later I became rather good friends with his daughter Jett Williams (his illegitimate daughter who had to sue Hank, Jr. for her half of the estate and her birthright). She looked just like her father. One night before we were doing a show together, she invited me onto her bus, opened an old guitar case and let me hold Hank, Sr.'s guitar. It was a special moment and I thank her for that. No, it was not like I knowed him all my life.

CHAPTER 10
104.7

"We listened to your tape and it sounds real good. But, you know, you're white and we're a black station," Vern Catron said carefully. He was program director and morning show host of 104.7 which played adult black oldies.

"I just want to ease back into radio, Vern. I know all the music and I like it. Don't you have something I can do around here?"

"Tell you what. I need somebody to read the news and sports on the morning show with me. I'll let you do that and you can start tomorrow morning." I thanked him, went to get all my paperwork done and started the next morning. Within three weeks, I was not only his morning sidekick, but then I did the midday show from 10am to 3pm. Lots of work and just what I needed. Our studios were in the CNN center and our sister station was WCNN, a fifty-thousand-watt AM station that broadcast Headline News from CNN twenty-four hours a day. Working was like being in the zoo with people looking at you through the huge glass sowcase windows all the time. We were adjacent to the Omni where the Hawks played, and the Georgia Dome, home of the Falcons. It was an impressive layout.

The Rodney King verdict came out while I was on the air during the midday show. Rodney King, a black man, had made the mistake after a traffic stop in Los Angeles of trying to break the fists and feet of some white officers with his face and ribs. When the officers went on trial, there was a fear of riots if they were not convicted of police brutality and whatever else they were charged with. Some of the beatings were caught on tape, so it should have been a slam dunk case. The cops were found innocent, so all hell broke loose. My phone lines lit up and I stopped playing music and just let all my black listeners vent (unless they had been to the CNN center, they did not know I was white). Vern and Bob Hunley, the general manager freaked out, not only because we were now a talk station, but a white guy was driving the out-of-control train. For almost three hours, I was sympathetic and understanding about their rage. Later Hunley and Vern couldn't say enough about what a great job I did. But the real problem had been exposed, "A whitie in the woodpile."

"I have no interest,' I told Vern as he was explaining that WCNN was going to go all sports and they wanted me to be the program director. "I don't know anything about sports, but I understand that it's getting uncomfortable around here having a white guy on the air. Just let me know how much time I have left and I'll find something else, no hard feelings. You guys have been great to me."

"Time is up," he smiled. "You were out of time when

you got off the air today. Now go on back and talk to Bob. They really want you to do this." Short career at 104.7, the one-hundred thousand watt mega black station in Atlanta.

> **PRODUCTION NOTE:** *Please insert Stevie Wonder's "Lately" here just because I like that song and I was off the page whenever I played it.*

Group, Friday afternoon.

Apparently when a psychiatrist releases you from the nuthouse and prescribes support groups and AA meetings as conditions for release, they take that stuff seriously. When the letter came, I was given a choice. Comply with stricter guidelines or I would be re-admitted to Southwoods for a lengthier stay. I called Dr. Chandora and apologized for the misunderstanding. He told me to report to Southwoods every Friday for group therapy and to his office every Wednesday evening for consultations with him.

Group, Friday afternoon.

The counselor was a jovial black man with a Jamaican accent. He brought his boombox and we listened to beach sounds for an hour in a dark room, while he dozed. We all assured him how much better we felt afterwards. We took a break so all the smokers could go outside into a courtyard and line their lungs with tar and chemicals. The rest of us just enjoyed the secondhand smoke. It was quite a homecoming. Many of my old friends were still there, and some new shiny faces We spent an hour tossing a beach ball around. It had questions printed all around it and when you caught it, you asked one of the questions like "what is your favorite ice cream?" Then everyone in the room gave their favorite. Mine was Moose Tracks. I confess, finally admitting this in a group setting had a cleansing effect on my soul. I felt they should have given me a token for coming clean. At the AA meetings tokens were freely given for almost any accomplishment. I got a white one on the first visit simply by saying I had stopped drinking, which I had not, and did not intend to. I like the taste of beer and whiskey. I only had to pretend I didn't for a year. I was surrounded by well wishers. New meat!

"Kenneth, since this is your first day, tell us a few things about yourself and what your plan is for making your life better," Christy said. It was obvious to the rest of us what Kenneth's story was. He looked fried. A poster boy for multiple pharmaceutical companies. He was wearing an olive drab coat, a camo T-

shirt and camo pants. Probably a combat veteran in the war on drugs, or maybe the war for drugs.

"First of all, I prefer to be called Kendini. Some people still call me Kenney, but Kendini is what I like because I am magical. I am here because my mother has a drug problem. I've always lived with her and she always thought she was sick so she took every kind of pill you can imagine. But she was a careful woman. She'd always give me the pills first to see if there was any bad side effects before she took them herself."

"So, are you here for a substance abuse problem," Christy queried.

Kendini looked confused. "I told you my mother has the problem, not me. I do still sample all the drugs I sell but it's just the right thing to do. My mother taught me that. I can't sell you pills that I haven't rigorously tested myself," Kendini said, looking at Christi like she was the one who was crazy. "The stuff I sell is magical. It can help you escape life. That's why I prefer to be called Kendini."

"Thank you, Kendini…"

"I'm not finished," he interrupted. "When I get out of here…if I get out of here…I plan to continue my career which is based on making people feel good."

"We're out of time," Christy said as she was walking toward the door. Kendini stared at her until she was out of sight, possibly pondering which medication to subscribe to treat that stick up her ass.

I had a chance to speak to Jerry Wallace as the session was ending. "Hi, Jerry. Killed anybody lately?"

"Where do you live?" he asked quietly. "If you ever wake up in the middle of the night and feel a couple of burning taps to the side of the head, you'll know I came to visit." I could see the perplexed looks on the faces of the homicide detectives…the smell of cordite and SpaghettiOs still hanging heavily in the air. "Looks like the perp jerked off in a SpaghettiOs's can, sarge." One week down and seven to go. That was the deal the doc and I struck. Eight short weeks and my sanity would be restored.

Group, next Friday afternoon.

"Belva, since you're new, we'll start with you. Tell us something about yourself and then what you hope to achieve during your time here." Mid thirties, I guessed. Dark brown hair cut so it hung around her face and blonde framing. That's when they put a streak of blonde to outline the face. She looked like somebody's executive secretary with glasses and a nice black pantsuit. Her face needed no makeup, thin but healthy looking. She was naturally attractive, with pouty lips. She looked more like a counselor than the counselor did. Christy was leading session today.

"I am a drug addict; I freely admit it. I like cocaine and occasionally heroin. I will smo e a joint sometimes but I don't like the way it makes my clothes smell. My family sent me here because they think I cannot control my urges. I work, then I go home and do recreational drugs. I've done that all my life. I hurt only myself. I did slap the officer who questioned me after a traffic mishap. He took me to jail and the judge agreed with my family that I needed to be here. I hope to find a husband while I am here, someone with similar interests as mine. I have never been married, so I think it's time." Larry perked up and stopped his simpering, probably wondering what she draws a month.

"Thank you for your honesty and openness, Belva," Christy sounded pleased. "I'm sure your stay here will be beneficial." Larry was still looking at Belva like she was a menu board at Burger King, ready to jump on the first opportunity to point out he was single at any minute. And that he and his grandkids had cut way back on their drinking but had no objections to a little recreational heroin. When called upon I always admitted I had been dishonest with myself and hoped to get on the right track. I never admitted to drinking still, or the fact that I had suicidal thoughts every day, had all my life. The voices in my head all complained about me. But, like Belva, this was my life and I had learned to deal with it, most of the time. Crazy doesn't take many days off.

I had a feeling Belva was staring at me, wondering

how much I draw every month. "Leon, since you're new, let's hear from you," the counselor said, reading his name from her list. He was about sixty, wearing a neat black suit with a black tie, the Johnny Cash look. His silver hair was thick and combed into place; he was clean shaven, had piercing blue eyes and was in good shape.

"I am a man of God and I should not be here. My wife felt otherwise. She said either I get help or she was leaving me. She's the only woman I've ever known in the biblical sense. I see this as just another test. The devil tests Christians all their lives. I would like to say I am available to counsel anyone here who feels like they need it."

"What does your wife think your problem is?" The counselor asked.

"Well, if you don't know evil, how can you fight it? If a doctor doesn't know what cancer is, how can he cure it? I was doing research into pornography, a curse on the world. She felt since I had collected so much of it and spent most of my time viewing videos and reading magazines that I was addicted to it. So, I am here because I am misunderstood. Jesus was nailed to a cross because he was misunderstood. Therefore, I am in good company. And if a husband makes certain requests of his wife, is she not bound by the marriage vows to abide by his will and do things he might request?"

"Thank you, Leon, but I see our time is up." The counselor left before he could ask her to do things, I guess.

I started to look forward to these sessions, so the eight weeks passed quickly. It was not comforting seeing people more messed up than me, but on a graduated scale, I think I fell somewhere in the middle, not as crazy as some, more so than others. It's a fine line between sanity and insanity, but it also depends on who is drawing that line. Violins are sweet and fiddles are just horsehide scratching on strings. There are lots of fine lines, lots of grays, few black and whites.

CHAPTER 11
WCNN, SPORTS RADIO 680, THE FAN

THE GLAMOROUS LIFE of a big-time program director/radio star turned into twenty-hour days, seven days a week, but I had nothing else to do, so why not? My morning guys consisted of "Skinny" Bobby Harper who had been in Atlanta radio for a lifetime and he had worked with Hunley at another station across town. Nice guy, but I knew he was not into it, mainly because of Harmon. "Charmin'" Harmon Wages was in the second seat, supplying color and analysis. These two never gelled and Harper took a hike within a couple of weeks. Guess who got put in Harper's seat. So, now I was doing the morning show, being the program director and going to games constantly.

I knew nothing about sports, but I did know a lot about radio. It's just entertainment. I dug in and read everything I could to bring me up to speed on current sports and the history of the SEC, the NFL, the Braves and some basketball. Adding comedy and wit to sports stories proved to be a good formula. Every level of sports fan could listen and find something they enjoyed. I surrounded myself with experts when I hired producers. Dirty Harry and George the Sports Geek were my two favorites. They had spent their short lives reading cards and watching games and were both gifted with the curse of dark humor. We were starting to have lots of fun.

"Charmin'" had named himself that and had played for the Atlanta Falcons. Before that, he was a backup quarterback for Steve Spurrier when he played at Florida. Spurrier won the Heisman trophy and Harmon took credit for it, saying he pushed him to greatness. Later Harmon was doing sports on Channel 5 in Atlanta but got busted for possession and distribution of cocaine. He did a couple of years in the joint and now he belonged to me. He was a late-night party animal, did no prep, and showed up right at showtime, smelling of alcohol and someone else's wife. Wait. Am I talking about me or Harmon? I didn't do that anymore, so it was definitely Harmon.

I hired a guy named A.J. Cannon to help on the morning show. I felt we needed something more than just Harmon and me fighting like an old married couple. A.J. and I clicked well with the comedy and voices, so besides just rehashing games, we started to have some fun. It was good to have someone attend games with me. We didn't sit in the press box as we were entitled to. We sat in the stands, drank beer and ate John Holmes hotdogs (that means they were big). We were sports radio, not like the dweebs who read the back of baseball and football cards all their lives, became sports writers and sat in the press box. We never watched much of the games, just the women who came to be seen. Did I mention that A.J. was crazy? He had lots of mental problems, paranoia being one of them. He felt someone was always after his job, which is true about all radio, there's always a thousand guys trying to get your job. We decided to rotate experts in his chair. We landed Chris Mortenson from ESPN (he lived in Atlanta), Randy Cross, the football analyst for CBS (also living in Atlanta) and lots of other high-profile people who were eager to be a part of this train wreck.

One morning A.J. was having a particularly bad day and he got into an argument with Mort about something stupid. Of course, Mort was right. He knew everything about sports, but A.J. was so mad, he jumped up and I thought he was going to hit Mort. Mort never came back. Randy Cross became our mainstay after that. He was a really big guy, so he had no problems with A.J. Mort and I talked later, but he never mentioned 680 The Fan again. Mort is a first-class guy.

Once things got successful, it was important for anybody involved to get their fingerprints on it.

"We gotta think outside the box now," Hunley said in his high screechy voice. Fingernails who made their living clawing on blackboards complained about his voice. He was a big guy who played offensive lineman in high school, so there were very few boxes he could fit in, so I guess he had to think outside the box. And having played high school football made him the expert.

"Bob, we're sold out constantly. Isn't that what everybody wants?"

"We gotta take it to another level." What about the box? Shouldn't we get that done before level hopping? All management primers 101 usually deal with this in great detail.

"What level is that?" I asked, looking for something sharp in his office to throw myself on. His expression went blank, reminding me of Earl. Our first year on the air, the Braves went to the World Series. The excitement was volcanic. I met Greg Maddox at some kind of social event. He's an amazing guy, but I was shocked when I shook his hand. What would you expect from one of the greatest righty's of all time? In fact, I often joked if Cy Young had been alive during Maddox's career, he would have been given Greg Maddox awards. Maddox's right hand was as soft as a woman's. I guess I expected it to feel like a rock. He was a master of control.

I became friends with Chipper Jones and he co-hosted many shows with me later. When I first met him, he had just been called up and was injured. He was the number one prospect at that time in all of Major League Baseball. And thanks to my guidance and advice, he had an ok career. (I'm joking for those of you who are a little slow). He had a turbulent first marriage. He married a girl named Karen, pronounced Kahran. "That should have been your first clue," I explained after we'd had a few. "Any woman who pronounces Karen like that has to be a total bitch." I knew a woman from Tennessee once named Suzanne and she pronounced it Soozahn. She was a total bitch. Case closed.

I was down on the field during pre-game batting practice the first day I met Chipper and we were talking. He was still injured. Tom Glavin walked over and said "What are you doing here, Larry? Do you know somebody on the Houston team?" Glavin was a prick, but okay, that was funny. Chipper's real name was Larry Jones. He became the face of the Atlanta Braves for many years. Bobby Cox was the manager during Chipper's entire career, and I talked with him many times. Cox always had beer on ice waiting after every game. Nobody cared until one day he had a bad night, went home and roughed up the wife, and allegedly slapped her and pulled her hair. The beer was never waiting after another game. I lost all respect for him after that. Not for slapping his old lady around, but for caving to all the beer haters. In for a penny, in for a pound. What do you say to a woman with two black eyes? Nothing! You already told her twice. That was our behind the scenes humor in radio.

We had a huge amount of fun with John Smoltz, an incredible starter for the Braves, but Smoltz was a head case. We discovered he had his shrink sit behind home plate, an area reserved for players' wives and close friends. The doctor always had to wear a red sweater so Smoltzie could spot him easily and this supposedly helped him keep his head straight. Every time someone called in to talk about Smoltz, our producer was instructed to play Patsy Cline's *"Crazy"* in the background. It was great fun for us, not so much for Smoltzie.

PRODUCTION NOTE: *Please play "Crazy" here.*

Football season is the best in sports radio, especially if you're in the heart of the SEC. I mentioned earlier that when you have a successful radio station, it's important for everybody to take credit, so Hunley hired a fatfuck consultant from Philadelphia named Tom something to tell us how to fix something that was not broken. On Saturday mornings during football season, I co-hosted a show with

Max Howell, a recruiting expert with lots of knowledge about college football. This was the highest rated show on the station. "We will no longer talk college football on this station," fatfuck announced in a meeting with Hunley and me. Now I understand when you come from a powerhouse college football mecca, sporting the likes of Rice and Rutgers, you might not utterly understand the importance of college football in the south.

"You're kidding, right?" I politely interjected. "And what do we replace it with?"

"The NFL is the number one sport in America," he said, showing his vast knowledge of something other than food.

"Not here. It's college football. And besides the Falcons suck." He turned beet red or maybe cabbage red since he looked like a big ball of red nothing. He decided it was time for lunch and invited me as well. He probably hadn't eaten anything in twelve or fifteen minutes. He excused himself to go to the bathroom.

"Good job, Bob." And I walked out to do some more thinking outside the box.

I think this particular morning we had been ragging on Auburn cheerleaders and the father of a current Auburn cheerleader was on the phone to rip us a new one. I had done this trick hundreds of times. When someone got totally out of control (or heaven forbid started winning an argument) I always said, "Go fuck yourself!" Then I'd hit the delay button and the last seven seconds disappeared, but the caller could still hear the missive on the phone. On this morning I did it backwards, hitting the button first and then telling the caller to go fuck himself. I had that sick sinking feeling inside when some new girl stuck her head in the studio and said, "Mr. Hunley wants to see you after you get off the air." Probably wanted to reverse the decision banning college football talk. Incidentally, we talked more college football than ever after fatfuck left. Guys who were never successful on-air in radio became consultants, experts telling the people who excelled what they were doing wrong. Consultants ruined radio.

"Goddamn, did you tell some guy to go fuck himself on the air?" Hunley screeched.

"Yes, but I can explain what happened," I couldn't have sounded meeker.

"I don't want a Goddamned explanation," he raged. "Now get out of my office." I could not believe I was not fired on the spot. If telling some guy to go fuck himself on the air is not outside the box, then I don't know what is!

"Allright, you caught me. Now what do you want?" I answered the phone instead of letting the voice mail get it. This woman named Liz Lapidus had called numerous times, but I didn't know her and she never left the required detailed message, which would further make me not return her calls.

"I want you," she proclaimed. She explained that she worked for a marketing firm and wanted to do a promotion with us and the Atlanta Knights. We already broadcast their games. There were never many hockey fans in Atlanta, but the ones who were there were energetic.

"I'll call you back," I said, knowing I never would.

"No, I need an answer now," she pleaded. "I'll buy you dinner afterwards at Jocks and Jills." Jocks and Jills was a sports bar located in the CNN center.

"Will there be beer and nudity?" I quizzed.

"Beer for sure. And if you want to take your clothes off, fine also." Smartass.

The promotion was funny with fans getting to throw pies at our afternoon guy Scott Ferrell of "Ferrell on the Bench" fame. He was our most popular host and the fans loved him. Liz kept her word and met me at Jocks and Jills. "I hope you don't mind. I brought a friend. This is Diane." I did not mind at all. Liz was cute, but Diane was about as close to a ten as you could get. I was thinking inside the box again. Diane was beautiful, Jewish, recently divorced, five feet one, dark eyes, long dark hair, beautiful face, figure, and a smile to die for. I will not give her last name. We were together for quite a while and I loved every minute of it. I learned to like bagels too.

"Hello," I answered the phone and recognized the voice and probably the smell of Lucky Strikes.

"Randy," she started.

"Leave a message at the sound of the tone and I'll call you back, "I said in my best phone machine voice." I had no interest in talking with her.

"Elain's been trying to get in touch with you. You need to call her right now and let me know after you talk to her." She left a number with an L.A. area code. I was finally cured. I didn't immediately jerk up the phone and call her. But I didn't throw the number away, either.

PRODUCTION NOTE: *Play "Crazy" again.*

Management hated Ferrell. He talked about drinking and even cursed on the air— all the thins important to men in their twenties. He was so popular, we started doing his show live every Friday afternoon from a bar called the Lodge in Buckhead. It was always standing room only; about fifty percent of the patrons were women. Diane explained to me that it was common knowledge that a good place to find a good guy was at sporting events. These guys obviously had disposable income and many were well-educated.

Fatfuck made it his mission to start managing Ferrell, limiting the length of time any one caller could be on the air, and limiting the content. This did not work for Ferrell. He was a comedy genius and brought humor into everything. He was an incredible talent. He left and the grief was city-wide. There was no fried chicken to ease the pain. Once again, a talented revenue producer was destroyed by a consultant. Thanks, fatfuck.

We were rapidly on our way to reading the backs of baseball and football cards on the air. Not the Hawks, because they rarely had even one moment worth noting. I made no secret of the fact that I was unhappy and everybody knew I was looking. I went to Dallas for an interview at a sports station but realized once I got there, I was burned out on sports. So, I met Diane at the airport and told her I wasn't sure about the job in Dallas, but whatever I decided, I felt like it was over between us. She was a sweet girl and good for me. I did not want to mislead her. She was thirty-five, successful, and ready to marry again and have children quickly. Her first husband did not want children. What did she expect from a guy whose mother never told him she loved him?

Hunley and I struck a deal that was agreeable to both of us. He got to fire me and I got some severance pay and didn't sue for the remainder of my contract.

Production note: *How about some more U2? "With or Without You."*

There were things about WCNN, 680 the Fan that I had loved and things that I had hated. The station was owned by the Dickey family, the patriarch being Lew Dickey who knew how to make money. His two sons, Lew, Jr., and David worked for the company because on a level playing field, they could not compete in an industry this competitive. Let's just say having "family" influence made simple decisions more complicated. Lew Jr. called me a couple of weeks after I struck a deal with Mark Kanoff, the general manager of WQXI to supply sports programming. After the golden days of AM radio, lots of stations were searching for the right niche to make money. Quixie had everything we needed, heritage call letters, penthouse studios in the ABC Capital Cities building in Buckhead and a fairly good signal. Lew, Jr. could not believe I was doing this to his family and threatened to sue me. My non-compete contract was over in about thirty days so I rolled the dice. They never sued.

I mentioned Dirty Harry from the old WCNN days and he was now my co-host. He knew sports and I knew radio (well I knew some sports by now). We started to make waves. Steve Hummer was a talented sports columnist for the Atlanta Journal and Constitution and he did a nice article on us after we struck a deal with Eric Zeir, the former Georgia quarterback, to be a regular on-air host. Christ Mortenson was supposed to help but he said ESPN pulled the plug on him at the last minute. We had him on the air by phone on a regular basis and that added lots of credibility. Randy Cross was also a regular host. Cross gets it. He mixes real life wit with deep sports talk. Chipper Jones followed and did live shows with us at a bar in Buckhead every Friday afternoon. We struck a deal with ESPN and they let us have "The Fabulous Sports Babe" on our station every day between ten and two. They even gave us five grand a month to help promote the show. Instant big-time sports station and the Olympics were just around the corner. Our main edict was we were going to have fun this time. To hell with the ratings.

We were not the Falcons flagship station but we were at the Falcons camp all the time doing live broadcasts and reports so we became a good go-to station to get their message out. This also gave us access to players and coaches regularly. With Kanoff's approval I put on a suit and pitched Coca Cola at their corporate headquarters in Atlanta on using our station as their official station. They would lease it and have total control of the programming twenty-four hours a day, so any visitor to the Olympics could tune in and find out what was happening all the time and of course live events would be broadcast continuously. I offered this deal at a bargain price of ten million dollars. They appreciated my confidence but offered only about ten percent of that amount. We never made the deal. Kanoff wanted much more. But doors were opened.

We had about everybody in the country who wanted to make a buck off the Olympics knocking on our doors. We got so many free tickets to high profile events that we were able to grease lots of advertiser's palms with them and they threw us lots of advertising dollars. Lots of these advertisers paid cash in advance. Kanoff's greed took over and he decided to change my deal, which meant I couldn't make as much money. I had spent a year there having fun, and then suddenly, it was not much fun anymore. After I left, the station became known as 790 The Zone.

CHAPTER 12

PINKY

WE ALL HAVE disturbing things in our lives. For me one of the most disturbing things I ever witnessed was the love scene in the movie "Deliverance." Another disturbing thing was Pinky Norton. His skin always had a pinkish hue, almost like he had just been freshly scalded, and he dressed like a dandy with suspenders, loud ties, pleated pants, shiny black shoes and a white panama hat. His eyes were close together, yellowish and his mouth was pinched like a rat's. His teeth were small, enhancing his rodent look. I'm guessing he was in his forties, had never worked and lived with his mother on Irvin (Irwin) Bridge Road. He could be seen often walking down the road talking to himself or to Jesus as some speculated.

Pinky was a queer and stories abounded about things he had paid little boys to do in local barns. He would often visit with Benny and Uncle John when my aunt and uncle were away. He had a problem keeping his mouth dried with the dirty handkerchief he carried constantly, almost like he was salivating all the time. He had a habit of pressing a thumb to the side of one nostril and blowing snot out the other onto the ground, rather than using a tissue or handkerchief. Nobody ever had to tell me Pinky was not right.

He liked Charlie, always commenting about how big and strong he was getting, the color of his hair and eyes and how grown up he was becoming. Kids usually can't wait to get older, so his compliments were welcomed by my cousin. Charlie did not know that not all Samaritans are good. "I always keep some cold Pepsi's at my house. If you're ever close, just stop by and have one," Pinky promised.

Benny's eyes lit up, never missing an opportunity for money or mischief. "If we can come to an understanding, Pinky, I can probably talk Charlie into coming by to help you with some chores too," Benny suggested and took a deep drag off his Prince Albert cigarette. Uncle John showed no surprise or interest in the conversation. He just stared straight ahead, fatting away.

"I'd like that a lot, Benny," Pinky drooled.

A year or so later we were camping out on the flat rocks, burning tires for warmth and light. Charlie confessed to me that he had gone to help Pinky with chores as Benny had promised. Pinky managed to tie him up and do horrible things to him. He left a dollar on Charlie's clothes, walked out of the barn when he was finished, then Benny and Uncle John spent some time on him. We both lost our appetite for the hot dogs, Pepsi's and smores. Charlie cried most of that night. My heart was broken and his innocence was lost forever.

There were rumors of other encounters involving Pinky, so most parents just took the easy road and told their sons to stay away from him. Pinky made the mistake of hurting a relative's son, and the boy told his father what had happened. The crime was never solved, but whoever used the double-bladed axe on Pinky never stopped until he was sure there wasn't a spark of life left in him. Rats are hard to kill anyway. Are you washed in the blood of the Lamb, Pinky? I knew for sure there weren't enough lambs alive to supply as much blood as it would have taken to cleanse that stain on mankind.

I did not attend the funeral or any of the visitations, so I don't know if there was fried chicken or not. Charlie, the once promising child with clear blue eyes, light brown hair and an easy disposition never regained his zest for life. I often wondered if he had been punished because of what he allowed to happen to Katrina. I also wondered if Benny had some help exiting the barn loft on his last day. And Charlie could cut twice as much firewood in a day as anyone else. His favorite was the double-bladed axe.

Charlie and I drifted apart, and soon I discovered girls and got a radio for Christmas. Life in Conyers, Georgia was still hard, and I was always looking for an escape, but as I got older, I just learned not to talk or interact with the people in my life. I put my family on a "need to know" basis and I know they welcomed that, at least Gladys, who called me names like "Mr. Encyclopedia." When I stopped playing *"Amazing Grace"* on the accordion on demand, the names she called me were not as kind. She had Earl, so losing me was no great loss.

Earl announced he was quitting school the day he

turned sixteen and no familial objections were voiced. He married his fifteen-year-old girlfriend and they wound up living with Gladys and pop for thirteen years. He could best be described as a juvenile delinquent, stealing auto parts from cars parked behind the theater at night when he needed a starter or battery, or just a new set of wheels. He wound up becoming a sheriff's deputy in Rockdale County for the last thirty years. I guess he's still there. We never talk. It's amazing. Many of the rogues I knew became law enforcement officials, and most of the dumb kids in my class became teachers. Small town life was never about escape for them, but then again, they had supporting families and were happy with what life had thrown at them. Seasons come and go and the best you can hope for is a roof over your head, food, and someone to love you. That's enough for most people. And the cycle of life continues.

> **PRODUCTION NOTE:** *Please insert Merle Haggard's "If We Make It Through December" here. A real downer.*

The scraping and digging started early one summer morning without notice or fanfare. Charlie and I (and my constant companion, Gladys Jr., who was like a wart on your thumb that would never go away) watched the work crews busily preparing Irwin (Irvin) Bridge Road for paving. The red Georgia clay was churned up, spread around, and packed back down over and over again. Before sundown when all the workers had gone and the big yellow machines were standing dormant, we surveyed the damage (progress) in both directions from our driveway. They had driven one by four boards into the ground, cut at angles on one end to make a point, every few feet on both sides that had numbers on them. We pulled up as many as we could because you never knew when you would need to make a rabbit box or just repair a hole in a treehouse or lean-to clubhouse.

We spent most of our days in the woods when we were pre-pubescent boys. No one ever panicked when they didn't see us for an entire day or an entire night when we decided to fish late on the Yellow River. Sometimes they might notice we were digging worms or collecting Catawba worms off a tree, so we assumed that they assumed the obvious. Looking back, there were just as many predators than as now probably, but they didn't get the publicity they should have. People didn't speak about those things, thinking if you never admitted they were there, maybe they would cease to exist. Or maybe there are just more people now, so you automatically have more bad ones. I guess normal children moved unknowingly from their innocence to a time of understanding the evils of the world, but our lives seemed to be defined by harsh realities that clarified the boundaries immediately between innocence and worldliness. I remember when my sister Donna first got her period. I didn't know what was happening at the time, but later I understood. Gladys screamed at her like she had done something wrong. Donna cried most of the day, probably cursing nature. Our family was not what you could call supportive. They never helped you through tragedies or hard times, they just piled on and gave you more difficult things to handle.

Earl was upset that day at all the screaming, but Charlie was kind enough to help him through this difficult time, explaining that one day soon he too would start to bleed between his legs and sometimes boys like Charlie and me were spared, but most of the time they had to cut your weenie off and sew it up to stop the bleeding. Charlie had an older sister and brothers, so he seemed knowledgeable on the subject. I often wonder even now if Earl has panic attacks monthly.

"What are y'all doing?" Dude Walker screamed at us. He lived about a half mile from us in a double-wide trailer across the road. He didn't work but got a check every month because he was disabled in some capacity (mental, I decided later) and was able to afford a nice trailer and a couple of acres of dirt and flat rocks. He almost lost his check early on, I was told, because someone took a picture of him jumping on a trampoline with a Polaroid, but thank goodness there was no way to verify when the picture was taken. We were pulling up new stakes near his property and were caught red-handed. Dude liked to talk, so he started in explaining the error of our ways and the fact that we possibly could bring on the economic downfall of Rockdale County by what we were doing. Apparently, the fiscal economy is tied directly to making rabbit boxes and repairing tree huts.

The dude was really fat, maybe three hundred pounds, and short, five feet four or five depending on what kind of shoes he was wearing. He had rolls of fat over his dark eyes and I wondered how he could even see out. He was holding a copy of the Rockdale Citizen in his hand and shook it at us and said we should spend more time doing productive things like reading. I didn't get a chance to explain that I had read almost half of the World Book Encyclopedia, because he was doing all the talking. "Just look at this miracle," he said as he poked a fat finger repeatedly at the front page. "They are replacing people's hearts that are bad with the hearts of people that have just died but their hearts are still in good shape." He paused, waiting for our gasps of incredulity. He continued by placing his right fat hand over the middle of his fat chest and said sincerely, almost tearfully "I don't know how I would handle that. I have a very tender heart and if they gave me somebody's heart that wasn't as tender as mine, I don't think I could handle it."

"We won't take any more stakes," I promised, trying to back away. Idiot. I knew this for sure and I was just a boy.

CHAPTER 13

WMRE

I WAS RELUCTANT to include this chapter in the book because it still causes me distress: my first near-death experience involving a jealous husband occurred when I was sixteen. As I mentioned before, I used to listen to the radio every night and practice being a disc jockey.

My father took me and Gladys Jr. to Monroe, about fifteen miles from where we lived to buy old bread from some guy who had a connection with the Merita Bread Company. He had out-of-date bread and snack cakes, which were surprisingly good and still edible, so we didn't mind the work. Pop bought this stuff to feed our hogs. They seemed to enjoy it too. On one trip, I noticed a brick building on the main road with a huge tower beside it. On the front of the building were the letters WMRE, 1490. I immediately tuned the truck radio to 1490. They were in the middle of the funeral announcements, giving details of who died, who they were survived by, when the funeral was, and other details. Organ music played quietly in the background. The funeral announcements were sponsored by a local furniture company. The guy reading the announcements was named Jerry Shane and he over-enunciated every word, out of respect for the dead, I assumed. (I later found out he had such a bad southern twang that the broadcast school he had attended made him over enunciate every word and he became stuck in the mode.)

"That concludes our funeral announcements," he said in a soft voice. A jingle played and then Barbara Mandrell's *"Midnight Oil"* started. Probably not the best choice after funeral announcements, but I liked the song anyway. So, they were a country station. I didn't really care, even if they just did funeral announcements twenty-four hours a day. I wanted to talk on the radio. By the way, I later learned that the funeral announcements were the most popular feature on the station.

After we fed the hogs, I called information on my Granny's phone and got the number for the station. A man named Verlyn Deacon came on the line and said he was the general manager. I told him I wanted to be an announcer in my deepest voice, but had no experience, but would work awfully hard. He told me to come in at nine the next morning and he would let me audition. He was in the market for some extra help. I skipped school and fired up the old Honda. He eyed me suspiciously when I told him I was eighteen, so I knew the jig was up. He went ahead and let me read some news stories in advance and explained he was going to record me doing a newscast. I was nervous, but I prayed to the holy Gods John Landecker and George Michaels, took a deep breath, mimicked the voices I had practiced for over a year. I pronounced every word correctly and was hired on the spot to do seven to midnight six nights a week.

WMRE had the authority to stay on the air twenty-four hours a day, but they signed off at midnight and signed back on at 6 am every morning. Probably old people were not interested in staying up after midnight. If somebody died, they could just hear about it at noon the next day. "Now, we don't play country music at night," Verlyn said. "We try to appeal to a younger audience at night, so we play top forty." I almost dropped to my knees and thanked the Lord God John "Records" Landecker on the spot. I was about to be a Rock and Roll DJ. And I was making forty dollars a week! Verlyn was heavyset, portly to be polite, and had a huge gap in his front teeth on the top, visible when he smiled. I found out later that he had a partial plate on the top and had asked the dentist to put the gap in it because some movie star had one and he thought he looked like him. I think it was Ernest Borgnine, so that tells you what Verlyn looked like. His pants were always too tight at the waist and the white shirts he wore with a tie looked like they were cutting into his throat. He had constant bad breath but I never told him.

PRODUCTION NOTE: *"Midnight Oil," by Barbara Mandrell.*

"You do have a license, right?" Verlyn asked.

"Yes sir," I lied easily. Was he talking about a driver's license?

"You need to make a copy of it and bring it in so I can give it to the chief engineer. Just go ahead and sign on the meter log and learn how to make power reductions and take the readings every thirty minutes." A guy who worked there named Ben Hill smelled a rat other than Pinky and explained you have to have a third-class license to work at a radio station. It involved a test with a lot of math, which didn't concern me. He loaned me his book to study and two days later, I drove to East Point, Georgia, took the test and passed, and was on my way to riches and stardom.

The next night my bowels had been working overtime, but the first time I opened that microphone and heard my name in the headphones, most bodily functions returned to normal. By the second hour, I felt like an old pro. I could cue records, read live commercials, play recorded commercials, take meter readings and talk just like George Michaels (I know, I live in a fantasy world. What can I say?). Later in the night, I started answering the request line and talking to teenage girls even younger than I was.

Funny. I drove my Honda to work every night and didn't get home until one in the morning, but Gladys never asked where I'd been. She probably figured I was off with some li'l ole gal. Apparently, Verlyn conducted a personal ministry on his own. Ben told me Verlyn had a wife and kids but was always looking to supplement his love life. Not the type supplements like the one-legged Watkins Products lady sold out of her car every month around the third. Verlyn would meet attractive women and tell them they had great voices and should consider a career in radio. He never had any takers for anything more than the free audition, according to Ben, but I will give him credit. He kept trying.

Norma Brock showed up one night and Verlyn had forgotten she was coming, so she sat in with me the whole night and we talked a lot about radio. Just doing my part to help the station manager out. She was pretty. Late twenties, well-endowed, shapely, attractive face and hair, and actually had a good voice. We became fast friends. She would come by lots of nights just to hang out. She and her husband weren't getting along, so she stuck him with the kids to pursue a dream. He had been older than her by fifteen years, so she had missed a lot of the things young people experience before they settle down. I was sixteen by then. She brought a six-pack of Schlitz with her one Friday night, iced down in a cooler in the back of her car. When I got off, we drove to a park beside the high school where her husband taught and coached football, basketball, track, and baseball.

I had had a beer before when I was around fourteen and continued drinking it sparingly just to feel older. However, I had never tasted beer on the soft red lips of a beautiful woman. And when I realized she was actually going to let me get her panties all the way off, I thought my heart would stop. I briefly thought about the paddles I had seen them use on TV in hospitals on patients whose hearts had stopped beating. I had seen people shot, people sexually assaulted, people die and people generally just be cruel to each other, all of which should have precipitated the immediate loss of my childhood. But somehow my childhood was still somewhat intact until that moment, lying on a blanket next to Walton High School, counting stars in the dark. Norma Brock sweetly introduced me to manhood. She stole my innocence (which is a lie because I offered it with no conditions). If she had said, "Now I have to stab you through the heart as a sacrifice to the God of manhood," (just like the Mayans and other tribes had done on the steps of the pyramids in Mexico and South America, information I had gleaned from the World Book Encyclopedia), I would have gladly put both my hands on hers and pulled that dagger through my heart. And then asked was that as good for you as it was for me? Little did I know that I would actually be sacrificed very soon, not on the steps of a large pyramid, but in a small radio station in Monroe, Georgia.

Verlyn stopped by the station late one night around ten o'clock and looked in the on-air studio and saw Norma and me, dangerously close to one another. (I stole that line from a Cheryl Crowe song). He didn't say a word, just glared, and walked away. You always hear about how bad it is when a woman is corned, but let me assure you, a gap-toothed toad can be pretty bad, too, when he feels scorned.

PRODUCTION NOTE: *"All I Want to Do Is Have Some Fun," by Cheryl Crowe would fit nicely here even though it's from a different period.*

When her husband called me the next night, no one had to tell me that Verlyn had called him and told him everything he knew, suspected, and totally made up. "Don't leave 'til I get there," the cuckold said steadily, coldly. "You and me are gonna have a little talk." No screaming, which scared the shit out of me. Quick, nurse, bring those paddles now! I went out the back door, stepped down on the kick starter, thanked God for those little Japanese people who had made such a dependable vehicle and headed east, leaving my Rock and Roll career behind.

Years later that station went out of business and the

FCC re-assigned the call letters to Emory University in Atlanta. W-M-R-E...Emory! Clever, huh?

I stopped by a large TV station in Atlanta years later to do a voiceover for a commercial. I had seen Norma on a show produced locally there and then broadcast nationally. I never expected to bump into her, especially in such a large place. She smiled and said "I've been meaning to call you. I listen to you all the time."

"I was afraid to call you," I admitted.

She laughed and said "That was over a long time ago. Stop by and see me before you leave." I said I would, still thinking about a blanket on the ground next to Walton High School in the middle of the night.

We went out to my car, a new Mercedes 380 convertible. She was impressed. We sat and talked for a couple of hours. She was prettier than I remembered. I still smile warmly every time I think of her and what might have been.

> **Production note:** *Billy Jo Spears' "Blanket on The Ground."*

CHAPTER 14

ELLA

I KNEW WE were poor when I was eight years old, on my birthday. Ella Smallwood (at the time), my granny and my father's mother knocked on our door and said, "Happy Birthday!" when I came to the door. She was smiling widely, displaying her gray false teeth, all the same size that fitted loosely and moved when she talked. She handed me a small brown box that looked like it still had particles of laundry detergent on it. It turned out to be exactly that, a box you got out of washing powders that contained a free washcloth in it. It was all she could do, she explained, but she was always good to me and I thanked her and hugged her. The washcloth was pink. I don't know how old she was or when she was born, only that she had survived the Great Depression and still lived like it was on-going under a tin roof with siding on the house that looked like it came from rolls of roofing materials. She always had a garden and raised chickens and pigs for the meat she needed and kept an old cow around and made buttermilk, everyone's favorite. Sweet milk was always the second choice in those days.

She was on her third husband, Robert Smallwood, a hard man with no fat on his body and no teeth as long as I knew him. He always needed a shave and his hands were as hard and course as the chunks of granite they dug out of the nearby quarry. He was younger than her, but I never knew how much. He always went to the mailbox every morning before daylight. One morning while still pitch black, a car hit him at the mailbox and dragged him almost a quarter of a mile, close to Dude's trailer. Dude was the first on the scene. I wondered later if he were heart shopping just in case. It was a mess, so Albert told me. He was still breathing when the ambulance came over an hour later. He died on the way to the hospital, broken up in shredded overalls.

There was a huge gathering because my Granny was well-thought of, a good Christian woman who never hurt a soul. There was fried chicken, my favorite, and some of thevegetable soup that she canned every year and stored in a pantry. So thick you could eat it with a fork. She cried a bit quietly and then went back to work supporting her hard life. She was sturdy, with some Cherokee in her, so the story goes. All she had ever known was hard work, childbearing, more hard work, and heartache. In the summer months, she always invited us kids to sit at a wooden table under one of the huge pecan trees that shaded her house. She'd cut a watermelon for us, cool and red. Sometimes she would treat us with a yellow-meated watermelon. I could tell that was her favorite. She would remove her teeth, stick them in the pocket of a print dress, washed out of almost all color, and savor the sweet yellowness. I always liked the red better.

She was my granny and she loved me. She never liked my mother and Gladys never liked her. They were polar opposites you might say. When she died, I remember Gladys standing at her grave, smoking a Lucky Strike and not shedding a tear. There was no one left to kill, pluck, and cook any of my granny's hens, so there was no fried chicken to soothe those of us who grieved for her. I thought maybe Gladys was upset about losing granny until I discovered her mood was spoiled because granny had left her house and ten acres (with maybe five of it flat rocks) to her oldest daughter Mary Lou. I heard a probate judge explain it once. "Nothing can break up a family quicker than a thousand dollars cash and an acre of land."

One of my few fond childhood memories was sitting with my granny on Saturday night, listening to The Grand Ole Opry on WSM out of Nashville, Tennessee. Later a friend of mine named Bill Anderson became the patriarch of the Opry after Roy Acuff got sick and could rarely perform. Bill told me that he introduced Mr. Roy one night and it was obvious to everyone that this might be his last performance at the Opry. His health and sight were failing. Before he started to sing "The Wabash Cannonball" his last time on stage, he heard the audience shuffling and people starting to stand up. He whispered to Bill and said, "They ain't leaving, are they?"

"No, Mr. Roy," Bill managed through tear-filled eyes, "they're giving you what's called a standing ovation." Mr. Roy cried too.

My granny would usually cry when she heard him

sing "*The Great Speckled Bird.*" I never got to tell her that story about Mr. Roy.

Production note: *Please play "The Great Speckled Bird" by Mr. Roy. I hope my granny hears it.*

CHAPTER 15
WPCH, PEACH, ALL MUSIC, ALL THE TIME

I WAS NINETEEN when a new station went on the air in Atlanta. Peach was a one hundred-thousand-watt beautiful music station with its studios behind Toco Hills Shopping Center on North Druid Hills Road. Andy Turner was the program director and morning host. If God has ever spoken to you, then I am sure his voice sounds like Andy Turner's. "The tape you brought is okay, but I want to record you here in our studios so we'll know exactly what you sound like and see if you fit in." He gave me a sheet of live breaks, commercials, and news to read over. Then he took me back to a production studio, showed me how to operate the board, and left. When I had finished, I opened the door and he returned and played the tape over and over and over, about six times. His expression never changed. Finally, he said "You sound better and more natural than most guys I know who have been in this business for over twenty years. You would fit in perfectly here. How would you like to do six to midnight for me?"

I was stunned. Most people work in radio all their lives and never make it to a major market. I was nineteen and about to be one of only four voices on a major station that was already getting big numbers. Only a small percentage of people ever make it to the major leagues in radio. "I would love it. And you won't ever regret it," I managed.

"Can you start tonight?" He asked.

"Yeah. I just need to go throw up a couple of times and then I'll be ready to go."

"Go home and get ready, then be back here at five. I want you to sit in with Jim Hutto on the afternoon show and go through everything with him. I'll leave some paperwork for you so you can get paid. Fill that out and leave it for me. You'll get paid every two weeks. I can start you at six. Is that okay?"

"Yes, and thank you again. I won't let you down," I promised. When I got my first paycheck, I had assumed he meant six dollars per hour. It was six hundred a week! I was rich and soon to be famous! I swore to the Lord God Almighty, John Landecker, that I would keep my life in order this time. And thanked him for another chance. Mostly women called the station. Peach (WPCH) was a major favorite among the fairer sex. I loved talking to them, especially when they told me what a great voice I had.

Twila Baker, so named because she was born at twilight in Los Angeles. I knew everything about her, at least what you could find out by talking to her on the phone.

I knew she was fat because only the fat ones had time to call radio stations. The pretty ones were all getting lumps on their heads from headboards. I swore never to meet a woman who called me on the phone out of the blue. Besides, she was twenty-five and I was nineteen. She also swore she was not married. I had become a pro at qualifying women.

Then the pictures came. Twila was a babe. Five six, one ten, long black hair down to her shoulders, shapely in the right places, big black eyes, petite nose and full red lips. She was dressed in black leather in the pictures where she had her clothes on. I broke into a sweat just looking at the pictures. We never exchanged phone numbers, my choice. We only had contact through the station. She didn't call me for several days after the pictures arrived. She had called me at least once a night for weeks. Maybe she was busy, her Uncle John might have died and she needed to make the fried chicken, or she could be breaking in a new headboard with a guy who had a better voice than me. None of the above. When she finally called, I asked where she'd been.

"I just wanted you to think about what you've been missing," she said coyly. "You are so shallow. The only thing that mattered to you was how I might look. You have just proven what a jerk you are." She hung up. I hate it when they're right.

> **PRODUCTION NOTE:** *Play the instrumental version of "This Way Mary." Can't remember who did it but I remember that was playing the next night when she showed up and got naked in the control room.*

"Are you sure you're not married," I interrogated her further.

"No. What is it with you anyway? We both know if I had shown up married, a nun and infected with contagious leprosy, you would have still jumped my bones anyway because of the way I look." She was right. "We've been talking for months and you've never once asked me out. I know we're close because we've talked so much. Where does this go now that your itch has been scratched?"

"I could take you to meet my mother, but I don't like her, so we won't do that. How about we take it slowly and see what happens."

"Ok, but no games. I'm not getting any younger." She taught sixth grade in Decatur and lived near the station. I lived at Wildwood Apartments in Decatur, only about ten miles from her, but most of our time together was on the weekend. She came by the station occasionally at night to bring me food and a quickie. My life couldn't have been any better if it had been created in The Magic Kingdom.

My day ended at midnight. My mind was still racing every night when I got off the air. Going home to read a book didn't have that much appeal. My aunt Alice always had a saying, only two things are open after midnight… bars and legs. I soon discovered she was right. The bar scene didn't start cranking in Atlanta until nine or ten at night and some bars stayed open all night long. While my little sweet schoolteacher was home asleep, I was drinking and exploring the darker side of Atlanta. I had everything I had ever wanted, a radio career, money, and a pretty woman who loved me. Why was that not enough? It was like I had holes inside me that needed filling. I guess those holes were poked in me during my childhood. I never lied to her when she asked me if I had been going out late. I never cheated on her. I had chances but none of those women could even come close to measuring up to what I had.

"Am I not enough for you?" I could tell she was about to cry. "Tell me what more I can do and I will do it."

"I am totally happy with you and our relationship," I said and meant it. "I think I'm just lonely all the time and have to be around people. I was lonely all my life."

"Then we'll move in together. I won't pressure you to marry me, but we'll always be together. I would hope that you would want to marry me later, but that's your decision," she said. "There's no pressure."

In every relationship, one person always cares more than the other. Sometimes the roles can reverse, but people are usually not in sync. And let's be honest: If I had married every woman I was in love with, I would have had over a dozen wives. I was not yet equating the fact that anytime I changed radio stations, I also changed women. Alan Sledge once told me a true pro can fit into any format. It doesn't matter what kind of music you're playing. Change formats, change women. I loved her, but I did not love myself. She was better off without me.

I had been at Peach for almost two years and I was bored with my life. I had heard there was an opening at WPLO, so I put a tape together, combed my hair, and put on my cleanest dirt shirt as Johnny Cash would say.

PRODUCTION NOTE: *Since I was headed to a country giant, how about some Waylon Jennings and "The Wurlitzer Prize."*

Christine Roach took me under her wing when I first arrived at WPLO. She knew everything about radio and the dastardly characters who infested it. She was pretty, smart and talented, a few years older than me. I almost pinned her one night on the couch at The Columbia School of Broadcasting where we both taught part time. She always kept in touch with me through the years, regardless where I was working. We met for lunch once many years later near Gwinnett Place Mall. She had been married a long time but told me she still thought about that night on the couch and sometimes wondered what if…. I did offer a do over, but she declined. She smiled and my offer didn't ruin lunch. You see, you can have female friends you're not sleeping with. But why would you want to? As Morgan always said, "If it weren't for that, why would you even talk to 'em."

*

The ghost of Fatma visited me on a regular basis, sometimes when I was drinking, when I was lonely or lying beside a woman whose name I could not remember. Just because I couldn't remember the name of the road doesn't mean I didn't have a good time on the trip. I wondered if she'd be proud of me now or ashamed. And I wondered why it mattered to me. Was I self-destructive or just a product of my youth? Already defective when I reached adulthood. Was I a bad person? Not as bad as people like Uncle John who was probably remembered by some in his family as the one who spent a lot of time trying to look up the dress of the angel on top of the tree at Christmas. Most of the pain I created was self-inflicted, selfishly keeping it all for myself. Quiet pain. The only cure was being on the radio where I could be anybody but myself. Tempus Fugit. Time Flies.

"No more the young hearts leaping in the dark…" my favorite Rod McKuen line.

CHAPTER 16

JOE

JOE BLAKE HAD done some hard time, three years worth, in Reidsville State Prison, starting when he was around seventeen. He never missed any school if you're wondering, having left formal education behind during the sixth grade to help on the farm. Everybody worked or nobody ate. He was my pop and I never knew much about him even though he was around most of the time. He was a quiet man, just under six feet tall, clean cut, a baby face like mine not hampered by much of a beard and he had most of his sandy hair until he died. As I mentioned earlier, we were on a need-to-know basis in my family so I picked up bits and pieces about his rough youth from different relatives through the years.

He got "sent off" for beating up a couple of guys was about all the information available. He was quiet, but volatile and hard from years of doing uneducated work. He was well-read and educated himself better than many who had bought lots of books. A pretty woman once told me,

"It's the quiet ones you have to watch out for." She had been talking about the rules of love. Pop was a different type of quiet. It took a lot to push him over the edge but, once pushed, he never stopped until the job was finished.

He was a bootlegger and used to dealing with people who would take your life if it came down to a few dollars. He carried himself well in those circles; I guess you could say he was respected in an unrespectable business. He was just under six feet tall and a few pounds shy of two hundred. His knuckles were large, appearing swollen, and the visible scars on them were not from a tangled mule harness, although he could manhandle a stubborn mule pretty well. Sometimes at night when he was making deliveries, he would take Earl and me with him, even when he intended to end the evening at a particularly bad watering hole like Mercer Mann's place in Lithonia, just a few miles from our home. The dirt floor was never cleaned, what's the point? Tobacco juice from Bull of the Woods chewing tobacco or Prince Albert cigarette butts would stain it again the next night.

My memory of the bar was just some boards nailed together and elevated by some unseen support system. Mercer Mann was one of Pop's customers, so you could get about anything you wanted there, legal or otherwise. Whatever your pleasure, Mercer was the man. Pop would always hand us a wad of ones and lots of change so we could play the pinball machine while he drank and took care of the customer service department of the family business. People react differently to alcohol. Through the years it always made me mellow and jolly, and eager to fall in love with the right or wrong woman (is there really a difference?). Some people got sadder when they drank, remembering a lost love interest or someone who had died. Some people drank just to numb their problems. And some people got mean when they were drunk and drank more because they enjoyed being mean. Mercer Mann's place seemed to attract lots of these types of fellas.

> **Production note:** *"Drinkin' Thing" by Gary Stewart and then "Misery and Gin" by Merle Haggard.*

Pop's hair trigger days were well behind him, but remember, once the trigger was pulled, he was the man to finish the job you started. "Them your boys playing pinball?" The big man asked. His head was shaved and this was before it was fashionable. And like most men who couldn't grow hair on their heads, he had lots of facial hair. Big mustache, bushy fu Manchu and Elvis-like sideburns. He was four inches taller than pop and outweighed him by at least fifty pounds.

Pop just nodded and said "Yep."

"Why you got 'em in a place like this?" He pressed.

"Look, I'm gonna finish my beer and we're gonna be on our way. That alright with you?"

"No, it ain't. I just might make a call to the welfare department tomorrow and tell 'em 'bout the way you raisin' your kids," he threatened. Even I knew the welfare people probably didn't give a rat's ass about how we were being raised.

"It's a free country right outside that front door," Pop said without malice. "You can do whatever you want, say whatever you want. But in here out of respect for Mr. Mercer and my boys, I'd appreciate it if you'd keep your hairy mouth shut." Pop turned away and drained his beer glass. "Let's go," he said to us. He never told us anything twice. We headed for the front door and the free country right outside it.

We were already in the car when pop came out. There was a bare bulb or two hanging so it wasn't completely dark. Pop never saw the hit coming that caught him in the back of the head. He went to his knees, grabbing a window ledge to keep from hitting the gravel parking lot face first. The big man followed up with a boot to the ribs, but it was like pop already knew step two of that dance, the procedure of dirty fighting. He rolled and the big man lost his balance and tumbled down. He never got up again. I was sick about the way pop was stomping his head and face with all he was worth. Earl and I were both crying. Blood was pooling around the man's head. He wasn't moving when pop tracked through a big puddle of blood and attempted to clean his shoes in the parking lot, cursing under his breath, not because he might have killed a man, but because his shoes were soiled.

Pop got into the car, breathing hard, and lit a Pall Mall. "Y'all want to stop by the Brazier Burger and get something to eat?" He started the car, backed up slowly, and headed for the Dairy Queen, not mentioning what had just occurred. We cried quietly most of the way there.

"Don't you ever start a fight," he said as we were picking at our burgers and onion rings. "But you better finish it if one comes your way, 'cause if you don't, the other fella is gonna finish you. There is no such thing as a fair fight."

I have no idea if that man was dead or not. My guess was he was dead. If not, then he would never be the same again. His fault. He went looking for trouble and found it. But I have never been able to get that scene out of my head. A man being stomped to death wildly by someone I lived with.

PRODUCTION NOTE: *"A Boy Named Sue," by Johnny Cash.*

Moonshine was made at night for the simple reason that it minimized the damage the county boys did to stills. If the still were running during the daytime, they could spot the smoke and they would be on you in no time with their axes chopping drums and copper pipes and soaking the ground with all that good white stuff. Pop was in the retail and wholesale business. He sold as much as he could to end users but he always made so much that he would wholesale it to other bootleggers who would cut out the inside of fenders of fast cars and install tanks all inside the car for transport. A set of good shocks was always a must because the cops would stop any car that looked like it was overloaded and too low to the ground. Cecil Friedman was pop's biggest wholesaler. He had several Fords with big engines and ran constantly between Georgia and the neighboring states. Cecil was not the brightest man you'd ever meet. In fact, the turnips on the truck he rode in on used to laugh about how dumb he was. But he liked to drive fast and he liked making money, so he was successful, meaning he had not done any significant time for bootlegging. He lived in a big house, drove nice cars, and always had money to throw around. Cecil also had one slight problem that disrupted his business model occasionally. He liked drinking what he was hauling and often mixed those two things.

I was helping pop load him up one Sunday night and he said he was headed to Montgomery, Alabama. It was drizzling rain and he'd been drinking a little as he called it. Pop told him he should wait until the next morning to leave. Maybe get a few hours of sleep first. He always looked surprised because he had big, bulging bug eyes. He was too skinny for a forty-year-old man and had stringy hair that always needed washing. He always wore nice clothes, but his hygiene was not a priority. There's a difference between someone who has a sweaty smell from working and someone who hasn't bathed in a while. Cecil fell into the latter category.

He hit a car head-on before he even got out of Rockdale County and killed five of the six black family members on their way home from church. My brother-in-law Albert always chased cop cars and ambulances just to keep up with what was going on. Cecil was banged up, probably saved because he was drunk, but the other folks were tore up pretty bad according to Albert. Limbs were severed, metal was sticking out of them and blood was everywhere. An eight-year-old girl survived but she had several broken bones. Cecil was given six months for the wreck and the deaths involved due to his intoxication,

and another eighteen months for having liquor that had had no taxes paid on it. You can take a few lives, but you'd better not try to steal money from the government. He had also named his supplier during the proceedings, so pop knew the heat was on. It was time for him to retire from his retail/distribution family business.

Pop was always tight with his money. Apparently, he had ratholed most of the money he had made illegally.

I think he had always felt bad about burning our house down so one day he, Earl and I went house shopping. We found a big three-bedroom house with hardwood floors, a full basement and a wooded lot in a new subdivision called Mountain Valley Estates. He paid twenty-five thousand dollars cash for it. We were still white trash, just living in a really nice house. He also bought my mother a brand new 1966 Mustang Convertible, light blue with a white top and the pony interior. It was gorgeous,

but from that day forward it always smelled like Lucky Strikes. If Henry Ford had still been alive and looked inside his beautiful creation, his only reaction would have been "What is that Godawful smell!"

Gladys always kept a clean house; I'll give her that. Of course, she made sure I always chipped in and did a lot of the polishing, cleaning, dusting, and scrubbing. I didn't mind. I finally lived in a place I wasn't ashamed of but was too mortified to invite any friends over. A shooting, a cutting, a cussing, molestation, or God knows what was always bubbling under the surface. Mrs. Brown, can Larry come over and spend the night? (Oh, and make sure he brings a butt plug and a bulletproof vest.)

Walter Mitty had nothing on me. I was a different person at home and at school. I was great at lying and covering up for the benefit of all concerned, especially me. I was a different person in every social setting. My life was a fantasy (not the good kind) from early on. I think that's why radio became so appealing to me. It was a mental escape. I was a prisoner inside the world I created and constantly changed. But, when I turned on the mike, it was showtime! I was always happy when the mike was on.

CHAPTER 17
COUNTRY GOLD ON KICKS 101.5, WKHX, ATLANTA.

"What do you want to work here for? We don't do any sports, except maybe NASCAR."

"I like the taste of cold beer, the taste of warm whiskey, the taste of pretty women and sad country songs. I am a qualified; my life is a country song." He laughed like he thought I was kidding. Neil McGinley was operations manager of both KICKS 101.5 and Y106.7, both one-hundred-thousand-watt country stations owned by Disney. My guess was he was in his mid-forties, short, dumpy (would have made a good housewife), thick hair, glasses, always shaved but missed a few spots on a regular basis and a man of few words. Hard drinker, heavy smoker.

"I've done a lot of country in my time and I need a job. Plus, I've already worked at almost every station in the market," I said cheerfully. "Besides, I've heard your stations and I'm better than anybody you've got on the air."

"Come in tomorrow. You'll have to piss in a cup. Can

you pass a drug test?" Obviously, he was looking at the resume I had emailed him and knew my Rock history.

"I can pass, as long as they don't test for Budweiser," I assured him.

"Yeah, me too. See you at ten tomorrow."

It was good to be playing music again and not sniffing jockstraps for a living. I had missed country music, I discovered, and dove right in headfirst.

Neil called me in for a meeting.

"Look, Mack Berry is sick. He's leaving. You know anything about old country music."

"I know everything about old country music," I said.

"How can that be?" he asked. "You're way too young."

"I started young. You won't be disappointed," I promised. I took over as host of Country Gold, and all the old stories came right back to me. After the first book of ratings, Neil called me in for a meeting. I was prepared to be relieved as host of Country Gold because I was too young.

"Can you explain this to me?" He dropped an open Arbitron ratings book in front of me with some numbers highlighted in yellow.

I didn't even bother explaining or looking. I just said "Look, you said this was just temporary. Just keep me working if you can."

He shook his head. "You got a fucking 12 share. There is no way. KICKS has a 4 share and Y peaks around a 2 share. This is a mistake. I don't believe this for a minute. What have you been doing different?"

"I changed all the music and I have been having live guests on."

"You changed the music? I didn't hear that. Just keep

doing what you're doing, but I am watching this closely. I am not going to die on this hill. Something is wrong and I'm not going to get fired because I can't explain it, and I damn sure am not going to say you changed all the music."

Same song, next verse.

"You got almost a thirteen share. Not possible in this market. There are over thirty stations with good signals in this market. It's impossible. I have been listening. It's an entirely different show now. Just keep doing whatever the fuck you're doing. The show is sold out and we're going to start promoting it heavily. And before you ask, I've got some more money approved for you. You will never be heard on another daypart on this station again."

"Why," I asked.

"Because as of right now you are Country Gold. That is your only job." And the legend was born. I rarely heard from Neil. I always threw myself in full force when it came to radio. Nobody worked harder than I did, and it always paid off. As long as people are complimenting the boss, all is well. I didn't need to take any credit for successes, but I did pay dearly for the failures. Wouldn't have it any other way. I still missed Morgan.

> **PRODUCTION NOTE:** *Please play "Gentle on My Mind" by Glen Campbell. That's Hadley's favorite song and it always makes me feel good. And when I feel good, all the voices in my head are happy.*

"The only other man who could make me cry when he sings other than George Jones is Vern Gosdin," Tammy Wynette once said. I loved everything Vern ever sang. He was a frequent live featured artist on Country Gold.

Besides being good friends, we shared another secret connection that he did not know about. I never mentioned it to him while he was still alive because he had been married to this secret connection and she had taken him pretty good. Her name was Beverly Jenkins, and Vern said even though she had cost him a lot of money, he got a few big songs out of the deal. Beverly's mother had married one of my uncles after his first wife left. Morgan and I were MC's at a show in The Silver Saddle and Beverly attended with her mother. Beverly and I had become good friends later after she fully blossomed. Thinking about how pretty she was, I still blush. Look up some old pictures from Vern's glory days and you will see what I mean.

> **PRODUCTION NOTE:** *Please play "Is It Raining at Your House" and "If You're Gonna Do Me Wrong, Do It Right," both by Vern Gosdin.*

As I mentioned earlier, Bill Anderson was the patriarch of the Grand Ole Opry. He was a regular guest on Country Gold, mainly because I loved his music. He was a good guy and a powerful friend. He could open any door in Nashville that I couldn't. I had access to every country star I wanted. So, it's important that I give full credit to Bill for helping make Country Gold a success. I worked seven days a week and spent about half my time in Nashville. Country Gold was no longer just a show, it was my life. "You can call or email me at Randy dot Blake at ABC dot com," I never had time to take many phone calls, so email was the best way to keep in touch. I could respond anytime and give a little more attention than with just a quick phone call. People were listening to me all over the world. I tried to answer as many as I could but it was almost a full-time job. So, they gave me an assistant. "Smart girl" Neil described her. She was supposed to be a big help. Not from here, he had said. Heavy accent. From somewhere cold. Student somewhere. Her name's something with a K. (Man of few words and fewer brains).

Disaster. Total distraction. Twenty-seven, six feet tall, thin blonde, the shape I like (or as Morgan used to say the shape I like, breathing, or not dead too long). Her accent was as cute as she was. Someplace cold turned out to be Sweden. Her looks could have lost us the Cold War. She was a graduate student at Georgia Tech, a software engineer. Said she liked country music, of course, this wouldn't have been the first time a pretty woman had lied to me, and I always reciprocated. Or as the great philosopher, Big Jim used to say as honest as you can be to a woman. I guess it was possible she could like country since all they had in Sweden was Abba. Her name was Kira.

"Great job. Now go home and get some beauty sleep. You might need it down the road," I told her over the intercom after the first show.

"I don't need it now?" She smiled through the glass partition.

"No, you're ok for now."

"When are you leaving?"

"Right now. I have plans as usual."

"What plans?" She pressed.

"I'm going to a place called Bud's Eastside Bar, have a couple of beers, maybe a shot or two and hope there's a pretty woman in there who will think I'm more handsome at closing time. Or a pretty guy...."

"Sounds fun. Can I go?"

"No, I don't think my wife would like that."

"You're not married. Mr. McGinley told me that. He also said you're a loner, you drink too much and you're a womanizer. He personally knows of two divorce actions since you've been here that cited you as a major problem. He also told me to stay away from you on a personal basis."

"Well, next time you and that sawed-off little prick are sitting around going over my resume, tell him I said… never mind." My mood was darkening. She was enjoying it.

"He also said you're the best air talent he's ever known," she confessed.

"He's still a prick," I mumbled. "Look," I continued, "I try to keep my personal life separate from my career. (Lie, lie, lie.) Here's what would happen. I'd have a couple too many, hit on you pretty hard, even though you're young enough to be my younger sister. And then it would be uncomfortable around here," I explained like the rational adult I was not. *Hello there, thin boy with a racing heart, longing to kiss a girl with lipstick on her mouth. I've missed you.*

"Can I ride with you or do I need to drive?" Pushy little thing.

"Drive. And if you get drunk, you're on your own. I am not driving you home." Stern. We walked into Bud's. Linda saw us and gave me a thumbs up. I shook my head and said, "Strictly business."

"Here's a dollar. What do you want to drink? Linda already knows what I'm having."

"Why did you tell her strictly business? Are you ashamed to be seen with me somewhere other than work?"

"Yes. At work too."

"Asshole."

"A truer word was never spoken," I agreed.

"Can we at least be friends? And civil?"

"Wouldn't have it any other way." I really wished Morgan could see this one. But why? There was no way I would ever get involved with her. Risk my job and my sanity? No thanks. "Liar," said one of the voices in my head. Thank you. I'm welcome.

Linda brought a beer and a bloody Mary for me and white wine for her. I introduced them. I could tell she approved. I shook my head slightly again. Kira turned heads when we arrived, men and women. Women look at pretty women just like men, maybe for pointers or to just size up the competition. She stared at me through rheumy eyes. I couldn't tell if she were tired or if her eyes were naturally that inviting.

"What's the dollar for?"

"Go put it in the jukebox. Play Garth Brooks' *'What She's Doing Now'* then Keith Whitley's *'Don't Close Your Eyes.'*" You can pick the third song. Wake me when your song starts. I'll be crying in my beer after the first two and may be passed out. I love sad songs. And please don't talk while my songs are playing. Just let me listen to them and enjoy looking at you." She smiled and sipped her white wine quietly.

My two songs finished and she said, "Bet you've never heard this one." Bertie Higgins' *"Key Largo"* started. I was quite a while and then I told her about Mel. Can't remember who said it, but basically, we are at our most vulnerable late at night. "The soul at four in the morning" was the phrase that came to mind. That's when we are at our weakest. Things are never as bad in the daylight as they are late at night when the darkness becomes heavy and presses down on your soul. We talked until four in the morning, closing time. We sat in my car for a while longer. I didn't want her to leave. I assumed she was just being kind after the story I had told her.

"So, are we gonna dance around with your hand on my ass all night, or are you ever going to make a move?" She said as she was staring straight ahead, not looking at me. I said nothing and started the car.

And then, a good time was had by all. We were rarely apart from that morning on.

> **Production note:** *"Fool Hearted Memory" by George Strait.*

We were married three weeks later in Ringgold, Georgia because you didn't need a blood test or much documentation there. The only requirement was that you were in love. She called her parents and they gave their blessing after I promised to devote my life to making her happy and taking care of her. I hung up the phone, smiling and crying.

"Are you sure? There's still time to back out. We'll probably lose the thirty-dollar deposit on the chapel and my father will insist on killing you if he ever comes to America, but we can just leave now if you want to." She had flowers in her hair, little white ones, I think called "baby's breath." I took her hand and promised to love her 'til death do us part.

I hated Nashville after that. Every man wanted her, but she loved me, so I was able to cope, barely. I hated anywhere I went from then on. I just wanted to stay home with her. We were inseparable and I was happy again. I even cut way down on drinking. I wanted to enjoy every moment with her.

PRODUCTION NOTE: *"Loving You Could Never Be Better Than It Is Right Now." George Jones.*

We were planning a tribute to Elvis. Can't remember if it was his birthday or the day he died. Everybody who was still alive was on board. Sam Phillips, Hugh Jarrett (Big Hugh Baby from the WPLO days. He did backup for Elvis when he was with the Jordanaires), Anne Margaret and many other people whose lives had once touched the King's. And then there was Priscilla Pressley. Kira and I were waiting to meet Priscilla at a really nice hotel in Memphis to plan her part on the show.

One of her "people" finally came out and announced "Ms. Pressley has changed her mind. She has her own career and does not want to detract from that."

I didn't know what to say. I started to leave and Kira said to the messenger "The beetch cannot sing or act. What fucking career?" Priscilla entered the room behind Kira just as she thoroughly summed up her 'career.' "She fucked Elvis. Big deal! Lots of women did. That's not a career." I laughed all the way back to Atlanta.

"I not only discovered him and signed him to my label, but I was a mentor to him as well," Sam Phillips said. "A lot of people forget Elvis was young when he hit it big. Just an old country boy one day down in Tupelo and a world star the next day. He came to me one day and I could tell he was terribly upset and nervous. I thought maybe he had some girl in the family way or girls. There was plenty of them after him. I finally got it out of him what was wrong. I said, Alright. Drop your pants and let me see." He finally did. It was just a risen on his privates. He thought he had some kind of sexual disease. I gave him some salve and he continued his climb to stardom." Sam laughed and laughed.

Production note: *"Anything That Touches You" by Elvis.*

Elain's sister Ora still lived in the Atlanta area and told Elain how to get in touch with me. I called her and we did our own "stroll down memory lane." It was hard at first, but we started laughing and reminiscing. All the old wounds were mostly healed. It was like a corpse that was overdue to be buried so the air could smell sweet again. I told her all about Kira and she seemed happy for me. At the end of the conversation, which I was hoping might never end, I said, "I love you, Elain," and she said "I love you too, baby. It will never be over." But I knew it was over finally.

Kira was the love of my life now and I had told her everything about Elain, the good, the bad, the ugly, and some of the crazy.

Production note: *Please insert Dolly Parton's I Will Always Love You," here. Whitney Houston did a fabulous version, but Dolly's is the best. This time it's for Kira, not Elain.*

The show got better and better, not because of me but because of the music and the constant parade of superstars who wanted to be on it. OK, I will take some credit because I did pick out all the music, but basically, I just played what I liked. And I was in love and I guess it showed. I never had to fake being happy when I was on the air, knowing a beautiful creature was waiting for me to chase away all the bad memories in my life. And did I mention we were rich? My Georgia Tech wife was a software engineer who made lots of money. What did she need with me? I offered to let her go anytime she wanted, but she stayed and actually seemed happy about it.

"All I ask is that you love only me," was her single demand. Something I had never been able to do before. Adam probably opined about Eve, "I'm only gonna be with one woman for the rest of my life? Asshole," said the voices in my head in unison.

"We're moving Country Gold over to Y106," Neil announced matter-o-factly.

"Why?" I was nervous. All that work. No just starting over.

"They want to build the whole Goddamned station around Country Gold. Y106 can never compete with KICKS, but according to your numbers, lots of people like what you're doing. And rumor has it, if you play your cards right they're willing to put you on a couple of their other networks. ABC-Disney was now a pretty big deal. Probably The Real County Network first. Big money, kid. Perk up. And we'll promote it on both stations starting Monday." This was unheard of in radio. It was taboo to even mention another radio station on the air, but to promote the fact that you could find Country Gold on another station…. This was incredible."

"The Eagle Has Landed," a big voice announced. Y 106 was now Eagle 106.7.

It was an oldies station for country music with Country Gold going deeper into the music than any other daypart. The first time he heard me play Hank, Sr., Steve Mitchell, the program director, almost had a heart attack. "You can't play that stuff," he explained.

"Why?"

"It sounds different." I was reminded of when I was at WPLO years ago. You could never play two female artists back-to-back. I was never given a reason, it was just a logical conclusion that some great minds, obviously greater than mine, had come to. You could never play two slow songs back-to-back either for fear the station would start to "drag." You could record a piece of crap in those days and if it was up-tempo, it got played. (No disrespect intended here for Billy Ray Cyrus' *"Achy Breaky Heart."*). I laughed and played more Hank than ever. The next week he was our featured artist for an entire night. There are lots of great stories about this man who died while still in his twenties and changed country music forever.

Mitchell didn't like Bluegrass either.

> **PRODUCTION NOTE:** *Please play "Jimmy Brown the Newsboy" by Mack Wiseman who had a perfect voice for Bluegrass.*

"I've got to take this. It's Loretta Lynn," I explained. We were having lunch with some of my wife' s friends at Houston's in Buckhead. In my hard drinking days, Houston's was always a favorite watering hole. They squeezed fresh grapefruits and oranges on the spot to make their drinks. My wife's friends had never heard of Loretta Lynn but she straightened them out by the time I got back inside. Kira really did like country music.

"Is she a go?" Kira asked, excitedly.

"She's a go for next week. Said she'd love to have us stay with her the next time we're in Nashville. She is so nice." I had always admired Loretta. She came from more humble beginnings than I had and wound up one of the most dominant forces ever in country music.

The Coal Miner's Daughter was a dream. She told long stories in plain terms and the country fans couldn't get enough. It was one of my best shows. Thank you, Loretta.

"Look, I'm not getting any younger. I think this is my time." I was in a meeting with Mitchell and the GM of both stations (I honestly can't remember his name right now). Sirius Satellite radio was preparing to do live shows from Nashville, so of course, they had reached an agreement with Bill Anderson. They mentioned they were considering doing a "Country Gold" type channel and Bill said I was the guy to talk to. I would do a daily four-hour show, program the channel and select all music. Money was not an issue, yet. They were willing to build a studio in Nashville for me. Kira was pretty much already on the bus.

"Look, we just need a little time. We're going to push through the Real Country Network deal and that's going to mean lots more money. You tell us what you want and we'll make it happen." I had never had an agent. Never believed in them. Now I was on the spot and could only stall. "It's almost a year away, anyway. I just wanted to give you plenty of notice so you can make plans. You guys have always been good to me and I appreciate it." They dropped more immediate money on the table and I told them I would talk to my wife and get back to them. It wasn't really about the money, just a new opportunity. Kira had put away quite a bit of money and it had made more money, so we could live for quite a while and not need anything. I had always promised myself that I would never wind up as a fifty-year-old disc jockey. That deadline was on the horizon in a couple of years. Time to spin or get off the pot.

Rhubarb Jones, the morning guy on Eagle 106.7 had always told me if you walk into the kitchen in the middle of the night and turn on the light, the little mouse who ran under the refrigerator was Steve Mitchell.

"Kira told me you called her, Steve."

"If you're looking for an apology, the answer is hell no," he said.

"We are not letting you leave. I just wanted her to know how much we want you to stay. What did she say?"

"She likes Nashville," I said, which was true. "She also said it's up to me." He was waiting for an answer. "I'm staying, so get the Real Country deal done."

"I'm on it," he smiled.

Since my house was burned down when I was a teenager, I have never been able to put down roots or even collect mementos. My roots were wherever Kira was. She also liked Atlanta as much as Nashville, but I never told the refrigerator mouse. We also had bought her dream home in Marietta and I loved it too because she was there.

I declined the Sirius offer and was happy about it. I had everything in life I needed.

Mel Tillis never took me fishing down at his home on Lake Okeechobee, Florida, as he had promised to earlier in life. I had seen Roland Martin fish that lake many times on TV. I think he lived there too. Loved to see him pull big bass out of the lily pads using live shiners.

Mel stuttered when he talked but could sing as good as anybody in Nashville. He was our featured artist that night. "You ever catch any bass in that old lake," I asked.

"Thousands of them," he said. "We'd get up early every morning before school and go fishing there."

"You ever miss any school," I asked.

"Never," he lied and laughed.

"Tell me a little about the song *'Who's Julie',*" I probed.

"I c c can't talk about it," he said and laughed again.

PRODUCTION NOTE: *Please play "Who's Julie" and "Send Me Down to Tucson," both by Mel Tillis.*

For the first time in a long while, I had a woman I could lie on the couch with watching TV and not think about other women. I could never understand people who collected paintings or rare coins. They were happy to sit alone and enjoy them. And then I felt that way about this rare woman I had married. The other shoe never dropped, although I expected it at any time. The only time she got angry with me was when I came in late and didn't wake her. Never do that. Always wake me. Suppose I were to die in my sleepand never see you again?

Cocooning. I finally understood what that meant.

"ABC's not quite ready to do the Real Country deal

yet," the refrigerator mouse, explained, "but don't worry, it will get done. You have my word on it." Hmm, the word of a small rodent who lives under a refrigerator. My career was safe!

"Don't worry, Steve, I know you're doing the best you can," which was true, although I also knew he wasn't capable of doing very much. Mitchell fell under the category of something I always included on my resume. References if needed: I have a long list of guys who have successfully ass-kissed their way to the very top of this industry.

"No coffee for me, no caffeine," she said at breakfast. "I'm pregnant."

"What?!" I was surprised.

"What, you think you can stick your penis in me as much as you want and nothing will happen?" She sounded angry. Then I realized she was unsure of what my reaction might be.

I laughed. "You are such a romantic. I was just surprised. I am happy. Kid will have a grandpa and a dad at the same time."

"Don't ever joke like that. I chose you. You were the man I wanted. Nothing else matters. I want to have the baby here, then in a couple of years, we will move to Sweden. I want my parents to know my child. I have a close family. You can go or stay here."

"That simple? You can go or stay?"

"I want you to go, but I know you have the life you want here." She sounded unsure.

"You are my life and wherever you go, I will go. If you want to go to Sweden, Sweden it is. Let's keep that part a secret so I can leave on my own terms. Can we afford Sweden?"

"We have lots of money," she laughed. "And besides, how do you say it here? My parents have more money than God."

More money than John Landecker?

The year was 2001, a Sunday night in February, and Dale Earnhardt had crashed at the Daytona 500 on the final lap and it didn't look good. I was already sick that night with a fever. I had been sick a while and tried to hide it from Kira, hoping it would pass. I read the reports we had every few minutes, then finally it was made official. The Intimidator was gone. Nascar had lost its Michael Jordan.

I opened the phones to let people just vent and express their grief. Every now and then I played an appropriate song like *"Will the Circle Be Unbroken."* Mitchell went crazy and called and ordered me to get back into music. I was sick and didn't care. I knew I was right and kept putting live calls on the air. He called the hotline several more times, but I didn't answer. He was furious, I was sure. Steam was probably coming out from under the refrigerator.

> **PRODUCTION NOTE:** *Duh. "Will the Circle Be Unbroken" by The Nitty Gritty Dirt Band.*

Two days later Neil called me and told me we needed to have a meeting. I was still sick and apathy was the greatest symptom. I was prepared for the worst.

Two faggoty looking guys in suits were in his office. Disney loved to hire gay people because they were neat and looked good in suits. He introduced them, but I didn't catch their names. He said something about ABC putting the Earnhardt show in the permanent archives, which was like a Hall of Fame for radio shows. I should have been happy, but I was sick. I just wanted to go home. "So, I'm not fired?" I ventured.

"Of course not. Go home and get well."

Ronnie Milsap was my featured guest one night and told me one of the saddest stories I've ever heard.

"Randy, when I was seven years old and blind since birth, my parents decided to send me to a school for the blind in North Carolina to possibly help me learn a trade or at least how to function in a world created for sighted people. It was a seven-hour bus trip they sent me on alone. Can you imagine even allowing your seven-year-old to walk down the block alone? I have never felt so alone and sad in my life." I was ashamed I had ever complained about my childhood.

I had met him in my younger days at a Shower of Stars show in for WPLO. In the afternoon someone remembered they had not ordered a piano for him to use, so I volunteered. I had married my high school bitchheart who taught piano lessons during the brief intervals she was not being a total bitch to me. She wasn't home so we loaded up her piano and headed for South Dekalb Mall. Thank goodness we were able to find a replacement piano from a music store in Marietta after it was dropped off the flatbed truck. The station reimbursed me. I cashed the check and spent it on more important things.

PRODUCTION NOTE: *Please play "Stranger Things Have Happened" by Ronnie Milsap.*

Bill Anderson holds a festival in Commerce Georgia every year. He's from that area and people come from miles around because the entertainment is high-powered. We were all sitting on Brad Paisley's bus talking to Brad about going to a bar to get something to eat. The place was called Shooters. Brad and most of the other artists were all late-nighters, so our plans were set.

Then a security guard stuck his head in the bus and said he needed to speak to me. I left to go with him to a back gate where someone was trying to get in, saying she was my wife. Kira was home, I thought.

As we approached the back gate, I saw a tall blonde woman towering over most of the people there, looking straight at me. Elain had told them she was my wife, but they still needed me to verify it to let her in. I walked outside with her and left Brad, Bill, Charlie Daniels, and others to feed themselves.

"I was home to visit my mother. She's sick. She's better now. I just wanted to see you one more time." She looked the same, felt the same. I felt the same. "I told you. It will never be over."

"I know," I agreed.

We sat in her car. "Do you ever think about me?" She asked nervously.

"Every day and every night," I admitted. She smiled. "If I were to say to you, start the car and let's keep driving, would you?"

"Yes, but I would have to take my kids."

"I know that and I wouldn't have it any other way. You see, I think we loved too much too early. We could never recapture those early days."

"Do you want me to start the car?" She was looking directly at me.

"I do. And take me to my car and let me go."

"She'll never love you the way I do," she pointed out.

"I know," I said, "but it has to be over."

"It'll never be over," she promised and drove away.

I was sick off and on for weeks and refused to see a doctor until Kira took me to the emergency room one night. They determined I had diabetes, or as Gladys used to call it, sugar diabetes. They gave me pills and a diet plan and sent me home with my long-legged fat wife (she never got fat, but her belly bulged). I think the long legs helped distribute the weight.

When the baby came in the spring, I was healthy and felt like I had just been born. Every minute with her was precious. I would often catch my wife looking at me when I was playing with the baby. She would smile and think you are the man I chose. We turned the house over to a realtor and bought another one sight unseen that Kira's mother had found just outside Stockholm.

Mitchell was crushed and then angry. How could I do this to him? I told him I was burned out and just wanted to ride off into the sunset and live like normal people. "We are not normal people. That's why we're in radio. You'll be back. Just call me when you're ready." I thanked him and he probably scooted back under his refrigerator.

I have met lots of famous people in my life and been to many places. But I traded fame and fortune for a small house outside Stockholm. If you're ever there and see a graying man on the street with a tall blonde young enough to be his daughter and a child who looks like her mother and could be his grandchild, say hello, and we'll have some hot chocolate and talk about old country music and what makes life worth living.

> **PRODUCTION NOTE:** *Please play The Last Love Song" by Hank Williams, Jr. It's sad, but remember what I told you, sad songs always make you feel better.*

EXCERPT FROM
THE DAMAGED MIND

By Dr. Shamir Chandora

I have been treating and studying the mind for over twenty years and have come to several conclusions. The mind is an ever-changing mass of tissues, that once they become damaged, stay damaged, unlike the body builders' muscles which are constantly damaged and then once healed, are stronger and bigger. Not with the mind. Often the damage gets worse and the rest of the brain can function around the damage but many times the problems grow. They can be masked and controlled with drugs to some extent.

We all live inside our minds looking out at our world. Everything that is important to us is created or destroyed inside our minds. True, we cannot control the process in many instances. The brain never takes a break, not even for a day or a week without possible catastrophic results. We cannot even say for sure where the mind resides in the brain. We know for sure where the thinking part of the brain is, and electrical impulses keep our body and world going, but no one can put a finger on it and say this is the part known as the mind.

There are commonalities among all my patients but each one is unique because of what his or her mind has experienced or learned throughout a lifetime. A particular case comes to mind and because of privacy laws, I will only refer to the patient as file number 680790. This patient doesn't recognize the difference between objective reality and fantasy and the lines are often blurred or non-existent. A traumatic childhood caused his mind to create a world where he could not only survive, but cope with daily life. Eventually, he had trouble even knowing what was real and what was created. To this day I have treated him with therapy and experimental and traditional drugs, but his mind seems to keep overcoming all the treatments and regressing to its earlier problems. It has been over seven years and he still decides on a daily basis what his life is going to be like today. He is a case study and has perplexed many of my colleagues, some much smarter than I. We would not have this case to study if he had known that there is no doctor-patient privilege when it comes to capital crimes. Murder is a good example. There is no statute of limitations on murder and when a doctor is made aware of this type of crime, he is bound to disclose it to the proper authorities. He admitted to killing two men, one by pushing him out of a hayloft and one he hacked to death with an axe. There was also a case of a missing girlfriend. He was questioned but never charged with any crime. One time he said she ran off to Los Angeles. Another time he said she was a bartender in Atlanta and just left one day, never to be heard from again. We were fortunate that he was captured at the Stockholm airport, otherwise, his crimes could have gone unpunished. We understand the murders he committed because of the background information he revealed, but to this day, we have no theory about his irrational fear of splinters, or why he whistles the same tune over and over.

> **PRODUCTION NOTE:** *"One More Day" by Diamond Rio. What the hell, throw in "Some Broken Hearts Never Mend," by Don Williams after that.*

The End

www.ingramcontent.com/pod-product-compliance
Lightning Source LLC
LaVergne TN
LVHW011828060526
838200LV00053B/3939